BOOK of legion

Scars & Promises

>>—💀—<<

ja huss

BADLANDS MC
BOOK 3

Property Of.
Infected Brand.
Angels and Demons.
The backside of twenty-three?

The cruelest thing HOPE ever did was show up.

SCARS & promises

Book of Legion - Badlands MC #3
A Dark Outlaw Biker Serial Romance

New York Times Bestselling Author
JA HUSS

SCARS AND PROMISES

Copyright © 2026 by JA Huss
Cover design by JA Huss
Interior design by JA Huss
ISBN: 978-1-957277-62-2
All rights reserved.

No part of this book may be reproduced in any form or by any electronic or mechanical means, including information storage and retrieval systems, without written permission from the author, except for the use of brief quotations in a book review.

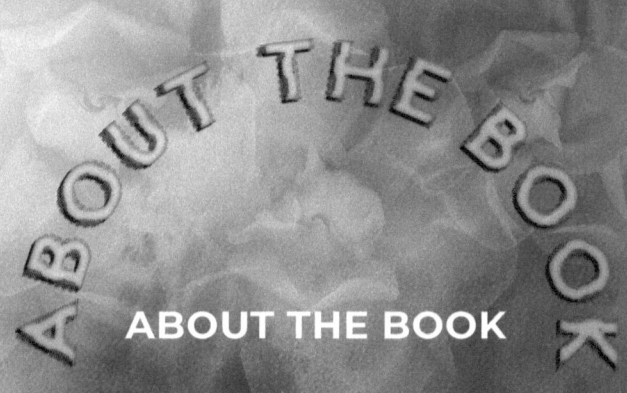

ABOUT THE BOOK

**Two families.
One blood, one found.**

Eleanor Ashby became obsessed with Legion Kane the day he was born.

The evidence is in the vault—thousands of photos spanning two decades, all bound up in a book with his name on it. Colt Ashby was supposed to be the 'good brother'.

But Savannah has to face the facts.

The Ashbys don't protect people.

They devour innocence and call it charity.

The Badlands MC don't even know the meaning of the word charity.

Everything is earned. Every act of kindness comes with a price.

Outlaws don't care about feelings, they care about brotherhood.

How far will you go for the club.

How much will you give for the patch.

It better be everything, or there will be consequences.

Property of.

Infected brand.

Angels and demons.

The backside of twenty-three?

SCARS AND PROMISES

The cruelest thing hope ever did was show up.

CHAPTER 1
LEGION

Everything slows down.

The way it always does when death enters the conversation.

The gun in my hand feels unusually light. Like three pounds of cold certainty against my palm belongs there. Has more right to be there than a spoon or a pen ever did.

The barrel points at Colt's forehead, dead center. I could put a hole right between his eyes from twice this distance.

My finger rests alongside the trigger guard—not on the trigger. Not yet.

But that's discipline, not mercy.

Behind me, I hear the clubhouse door creak open. Boots on gravel.

In front of me, Colt's eyes widen just enough to show he understands exactly how close he is to the end of his story.

My arm doesn't shake. Prison built these muscles

layer by layer, cell by cell. Three years of push-ups and pull-ups until my body became a weapon that didn't need to be smuggled in.

Destiny clutches her baby tighter, the yellow blanket bright against the gathering dusk. "Legion, don't—"

"Shut up," I say, voice flat. Not angry. Just empty.

My focus narrows to Colt's face, but my mind splits open, falling backward through time.

Once upon a time, Destiny was my world. When she was small. Hours old. Days old. Weeks old. Hell, my fascination with Destiny Kane lasted several years. I was fifteen when she was born.

Before Destiny, it was just me and mama. When Deacon, Destiny and Mercy's father, started hanging around, I thought things would never be good again. Not that they were much better before, but a single boy to take care of is one thing. A boy and two girls paints a very different picture of what it means to survive.

But it wasn't all bad. Deacon didn't hang around much after Destiny was born. He worked, spent most of his money on gambling, came home at night to fuck my mama, sleep, and eat our food. But he helped, I guess.

Destiny was the most beautiful child ever. She's got a more exotic look to her compared to me. Dark hair, almost midnight black, where mine has always been blond. But we both have mama's blue eyes.

There were days back when she was small where I would just look at her. Get lost in that beauty. In my limited world of scrubland and lonely prairies, Destiny was a bluebell surrounded by dust.

Then Mercy came and it all fell apart.

One kid a single mother can handle. Even one like me.

Two... it's iffy.

Three breaks everythin'.

Deacon's angry indifference, combined with the demands of hungry children—well, it was too much for her.

Did my mama kill herself? Did her car slip off that icy freeway overpass on purpose, or by accident?

Won't ever know.

But did she choose to take enough oxy to kill a horse that same night, leave her newborn baby home alone, and then go out drivin' in a blizzard?

That's a resoundin' yes, folks.

I won't let Destiny's life end up being so worthless.

I can't do it. I won't be able to live with myself if her end is nothin' but a repeat of the woman who brought her into this world.

The wind picks up, blowing grit across the parking lot. It stings my eyes, but I don't blink. The late afternoon sun sits heavy and gold on the horizon, casting long shadows across Colt's face. Sweat beads along my hairline, trickling down my temple.

My world has always been about choices with no good options.

Prison or my sisters.

Club or Savannah.

Now this—Destiny with Colt's baby, my gun, my sister, my woman, my club.

Thirty-nine men behind these walls just voted to protect what's mine. But Destiny's mine too. Blood of my blood. The one I failed by going inside, by not being there when she needed me.

I don't need to ask to know that every member of Badlands is rethinking that decision now.

Even Diesel. He's my best friend, but this right here—this intrusion, this drama, this... impossible situation with Destiny and Colt...

Church, and the decisions that come out of it, aren't about friendship.

They're about survival.

The skin between my shoulder blades prickles and I can feel those eight pairs of dissenting eyes boring into my back like bullet holes. I don't need to turn around to know exactly who's watching—because *everyone* is watching.

The shift in the air behind me is subtle. The moment when respect starts bleeding into doubt. Every second this gun stays raised, I'm burning through the goodwill my three years inside earned me.

The brand on my chest throbs with my heartbeat, still raw, still healing.

What does it mean, it's asking.

What am I willing to give up to respect that brand.

I'm at a crossroads here. Every single member of Badlands is watching. Waiting to see which Legion Kane I really am.

The disciplined soldier who earned his patch in blood and silence?

Or a fool who'll burn it all down for a woman and a sister?

The fact is, in this moment, I'm not really sure.

"Give me one reason," I say to Colt, "why I shouldn't

paint this parking lot with whatever's inside your skull."

The baby makes a small sound—not quite a cry, just a reminder it exists. That it didn't ask to be born into this war.

Destiny Kane used to be all sharp edges—black eyeliner so thick it looked painted on with a Sharpie, red lipstick smeared like a wound, hair dyed whatever color she could steal from the drugstore that week. A walking "fuck you" to the world that made her.

This girl standing in front of me looks like she walked straight off Savannah's Instagram. Her hair is clean and shiny, falling over her shoulders in soft waves. No makeup except something that makes her skin glow. She's wearing a white sundress with tiny flowers on it. Like motherhood washed all the rage out of her and left something fragile behind.

She's thinner though. Hollow in the cheeks where there should be fullness. Her eyes dart between my face and the gun I'm still holding on Colt.

The baby protests again, and Destiny shifts the bundle in her arms. "Do you want to meet your niece?" Her voice is quiet, careful. Not the Destiny I remember at all.

I don't answer. Can't answer. But she takes a step forward anyway, pulling back the yellow blanket.

"Her name's Marigold. Marigold Ashby."

The baby blinks up at me with dark blue eyes. Blonde wisps of hair catch the light. She doesn't look anything like my sister.

She looks like Savannah.

Something twists in my chest, hard and painful. This

child isn't a Kane. She's an Ashby through and through. Golden and perfect where we've always been dirt and struggle.

Even me. This gold hair of mine has always been the other side of clean. Never bright like the sun, but tinted with shadows.

My eyes snap back to Colt, and I breathe through my anger. "She's seventeen, you piece of shit. You fucking preyed on my little sister while I was locked up? While she was alone? What kind of goddamn animal—"

"Legion." Destiny's voice cuts through my rage. "I'm eighteen now." I look at her, but my aim stays true on Colt's forehead. "Why do you think I waited until today to come find you?" she continues, bouncing the baby gently when she starts to fuss. "I'm legal now. That part of the drama is over."

Eighteen now...

It takes me a moment to understand what she's really saying.

Eighteen now...

Today is her birthday.

And I forgot.

I've been so wrapped up in Savannah, in the club, in my own shit that I didn't even remember my own sister's birthday.

Hell, I didn't even go look for her. Didn't even ride down to the damn truck stop and look around.

The weight of my failure sits heavy on my shoulders. I was supposed to protect her. Keep her safe. Instead, I went to prison and left her alone, and an Ashby—a fucking Ashby—stepped in to take my place.

I look at the baby again. My niece. Conceived while I was still inside, counting days on a cinder block wall.

I want to hate this child. Want to see her as proof of everything I couldn't prevent.

But she's just a baby. Innocent. Perfect little fingers curling against the blanket. A Kane by blood, no matter what her last name is.

And despite everything, despite the gun in my hand and the rage in my chest, I feel something protective unfurl inside me at the sight of her tiny face.

"Why'd you run, Des?" My voice is quieter now, but I keep the gun steady on Colt. "Why'd you just disappear?"

She glances at Colt before answering. "Cash found out. About the baby. About us." Her hand tightens on the blanket. "He came to the trailer one night when you were inside. Said some things."

"What things?" These words fall out as rage.

"That no Kane was gonna dilute Ashby blood. That he'd make sure I never kept it." Her eyes harden, and there's my sister again, buried beneath the sundress. "Said he'd take care of it personally."

My finger twitches against the trigger. Colt must notice because he raises his hands slightly higher. "I stepped in. Got her out—"

"You got her *out*?" I am nothing but demons now. "You got her *out*? You piece of shit! You knocked her *up*. How fucking old—" I do some quick math. Seventeen minus three years inside equals... rage, that's what it equals. "Fourteen," I say. She was fourteen when I went in." I'm growling now. "She was a child and you—"

"Child," Destiny sneers. "Stop it. I haven't been a

child since Mama died when I was eight. You left me." She's the one growlin' now. "For *them*." She nods her head at the men behind me.

Fuck.

"You did time for them, Legion. Time you didn't even owe. Time they stole, not just from you, but from *me*."

"Shut up, Destiny."

"*Shut up, Destiny*," she mocks back. "No, Legion. I will not shut up."

"Can I just explain," Colt says.

"Fuck off," I snarl. "No one's talking to you, Colt."

But he doesn't fuck off, and Destiny—who has never been afraid of me a single moment of her entire life—takes over. "We met at the library," she says, bouncing the baby when she fusses. "I was looking through college catalogs online. Community college stuff. Thinking maybe…" She trails off, that dream already fading. "Colt was having a meeting with the librarians. Something about organizing a show for Eleanor's photographs and…"

Eleanor.

The name hits me like a fist to the face. Unexpected. Eleanor Ashby with her camera always pointed at me. From the time I was small enough to fit in the viewfinder, she was there. Watching. Documenting.

I see her in flashes—the way she'd adjust the light with her hands like she was sculpting it. How she'd tell me to hold still, just one more, just like that. The smell of her perfume when she'd get close to position my chin just right.

But that was later. Much later. That's not how it started.

It started with her showing up at my school, dropping off a bagged lunch. Sandwiches. She even cut the crusts off. Nobody ever cut my crusts off.

I can't even count up the number of times Eleanor Ashby showed up at Drybone Elementary with a bag of food at noon. It must've been hundreds, though. Hundreds of times.

But the number of times she found my face in the lens of her camera must've surely numbered in the thousands.

She took tens of thousands of photos of me.

It wouldn't even surprise me if, after everything was all accounted for, she took more of me than she did Savannah.

She'd slip me twenty-dollar bills sometimes. Tell me it was for modeling. Make me promise not to tell no one.

Which, ya know, is your first clue that something isn't right.

But none of it ever *felt* wrong.

That's the problem with wrongness, I guess. It rides a line.

I didn't understand what was goin' on back then, and I still don't fully understand it now.

The confusion must show on my face because Destiny's voice suddenly cuts through my thoughts. "—and that's how we started seeing each other. Legion? Are you even listening?"

I blink, realizing I've missed something important.

Some critical piece of how my underage sister ended up pregnant by an Ashby while I was locked in a cell.

"What do you want from me?" I ask, refocusing on the present. "Why come here now?"

Colt answers this time, his voice steady despite the gun still aimed at his head. "Nothing. We're leaving town tonight. Heading west. I just thought..." He glances at Destiny. "We thought you should meet your niece before we go. That's all."

"That's all," I repeat, the words hollow.

"It's a good place," Destiny adds, shifting the baby to her other hip. "Somewhere I've always wanted to go."

I squint at her, because she's looking me dead in the eyes when these words come out.

Some place I've always wanted to go.

And just like that, I'm back in our old trailer. Destiny, little then, taping pictures cut from magazines to the wall above her mattress on the floor. Snow-capped mountains. Log cabins with smoke curling from stone chimneys. Lake that looked like glass.

There are lots of pretty places in Montana. Like... thousands, probably. Hell, even Drybone, with its proximity to Glendive and Makoshika State Park, has breathtakingly beautiful places all around it.

But Destiny only had eyes for the Tetons.

Jackson Hole, Wyoming.

"I'm gonna live there one day." She must've told me that a hundred times as she looked at the pictures on her wall. "In a big fancy house made of logs."

I remember nodding along. Telling her she could go anywhere she wanted.

Until I didn't.

Three days before I took the fall for the club, I snapped at her. "That's not a place for us, Destiny. Only rich people live there." I tore down one of her pictures. "People like us don't get happy endings in places like that. We get trailer parks and prison sentences. That's our inheritance."

God, I'm a dick.

I don't say Jackson Hole out loud now. Not that I'm hedging my bets on my brothers behind me, but the less they know about this, the better. What Destiny just told me was a code, so that's how it's gonna stay.

They're not just on the run from Cash and whatever Ashby bullshit will follow them forever now that a bloodline baby is involved, they're runnin' from me too.

My arm is starting to ache from holding the gun level. My ribs scream every time I inhale, my head is poundin' like a motherfucker. *Everything* hurts.

The baby makes a soft sound, like a question.

I lower the gun slowly, muscle by muscle, like I'm dismantling a bomb. The metal feels heavier going down than it did coming up. Like gravity knows what this surrender costs me.

The gun points at the ground now. Not holstered. Not surrendered. Just... paused.

Destiny cradles the baby against her chest. Her eyes are different now—softer around the edges but harder at the center. Motherhood didn't make her gentle. Just gave her something worth fighting for.

"I hope..." she says, voice catching a little. "I hope one day, you slay that demon, Legion. I really do."

The words hit hard. A stab in the back. A shiv in the ribs. Not because she said them, but because she means them. Like *I'm* the one possessed. Like *I'm* the one who needs saving here.

My name is Legion, for we are many. The verse I've carried since birth, tattooed across my soul before it ever touched my skin.

Destiny shifts the baby in her arms, takes a step toward me. "You want to hold her? Just once before—"

"*No.*" The word comes out rough, unfinished.

"She's blood, Legion. Your blood."

I shake my head, backing away like she's fire.

This baby is doomed. Adding my filth to her burden will only make it happen faster.

And then, in this moment of damnation that feels like it was handcrafted just for me, Colt opens the Range Rover door. Destiny hesitates, looking back at me one last time before climbing in. Colt gets in too. The engine purrs to life—wealth sounds different, even in machinery.

They back up, do a three-point turn, and then pull away slowly. Tires crunching gravel, kicking up dust that hangs in the air like unspoken apologies.

I watch until they disappear around the bend.

Failure settles in my gut like concrete.

I never protected her.

And now I never will.

I slide the gun down into the small of my back as I walk across the compound. Every boot step feels like regret. Forty-seven pairs of eyes watch me from everywhere imaginable. Windows. Doorways. Shadows. Some with respect, some with judgment, all measuring what just happened against what they would've done.

Brick stands by the door, face giving nothing away except the slight nod—acknowledgment, not approval. Diesel's jaw works like he's chewing on words he won't spit out. Roach just stares, calculating odds I don't want to know.

The clubhouse looks different now. Smaller. The air thicker with something unspoken. The same walls and floors, but the brotherhood has shifted. The vote bought Savannah protection, but what just happened put cracks in foundations I can't see.

Savannah's eyes find mine—questions I don't have answers for written across her face. She's on the porch, standing behind Mama Jo and the others like she's been hiding.

I walk past her without slowing. The gun at the small of my back feels heavier than it should.

The threshold looms ahead—just a doorway, just worn wood and metal hinges. But crossing it feels like choosing sides.

In or out.

Brother or blood.

Club or family.

I step through, feeling something tear inside me as I do.

Something that won't heal clean and I'll never get back.

CHAPTER 2
SAVANNAH

The blood beneath my tattoo bandage pulses with each heartbeat. Fresh ink, fresh claim—the words "PROPERTY OF DEMON" still pressing into the clear wrap.

The Range Rover disappears, leaving a cloud of dust behind as Colt drives away with my niece. Legion's niece.

Our niece.

I'm not sure that makes sense yet.

I'm not sure anything makes sense these days.

Watching Legion point a gun at my youngest brother didn't evoke the kind of reaction it should've.

He was calm. His hand did not shake, not one bit. There was no wild, jittery aim of someone who might miss, but the practiced calm of someone who never does. The way men who understand consequences handle death when the possibility of it rises up in front of them.

I should've felt fear for Colt. I should've felt sympathy for Destiny.

But God help me, watching Legion handle that gun made something low in my belly tighten.

Not because I wanted Colt dead—though part of me might after what I just learned—but because Legion in control is violence made beautiful.

In another timeline, I would have been Destiny's sister-in-law.

In that timeline, I would marry Legion instead of running away to college in order to put off the reality of Ashby expectations.

But I don't live in that timeline, I live in this one. The one where I came back to mama and the ranch, and the camera.

The one where Legion went to prison for something he didn't do.

The one where my thirty-one-year-old brother got his seventeen-year-old sister knocked up.

Now we're strangers connected by a child who shouldn't exist.

I'm ashamed for Colt, though Colt didn't look the least bit ashamed of himself. Standing there in his designer clothes next to Destiny in her sundress, like they're playing house instead of running from the wreckage they've created.

Legion turns from the empty road, dust settling around his boots as he walks back toward the clubhouse. Toward me. His eyes find mine for just a heartbeat. No words, just a look that says everything and nothing at all.

The space between us stretches wide as prairie sky

though I could reach out and touch him if I dared. But I don't. His jaw is set in that way that means he's already gone, already somewhere I can't follow.

He disappears into the clubhouse without slowing, and I'm left standing on the porch with my bleeding wrist and my Badlands jacket, feeling the weight of choices made and unmade, settling into my bones.

My mother would've framed this moment differently.

Eleanor Ashby would've posed me just so—chin lifted, eyes reflecting the dying light, my hand reaching after something I can't have. She would've called it art instead of heartbreak.

The memory of finding her secret rushes in, unbidden and unwanted. It happened after the reading of the will that made me both prisoner and queen of everything she built. The brass key the lawyer slid across his expansive mahogany desk. With a very serious expression, he said it was for my eyes only.

That night, I'd climbed the stairs to her study—the one place in the house where the light always felt wrong. Cold. The wooden box behind her awards was inlaid with mother-of-pearl. Inside, a note with numbers. Not coordinates, though they might as well have been. They led me down, down, down.

The elevator hidden in my closet. The vault thirty feet below where the ranch's bedrock starts.

Eleanor Ashby's photograph archive.

I'd been down there, but never alone. Never allowed to wander or look through things. Mother kept her negatives in perfect archival condition—every single photo she ever took. So it was exciting to finally have the code to use the elevator and see the photos without supervision.

But it was the safe that called to me. Heavy steel, turn of the century.

I'd been staring at that safe in the corner for decades before I finally had the means to open it.

The book was leather-bound, hand-stitched. Gorgeous. Inside and out.

Toddler Legion looked like a wild angel. An angel about to be thrown from grace, even at that tender age. Blond hair sticking up wild, a toy truck clutched in his fist. His eyes already knew things children shouldn't. His face was dirty, but somehow Eleanor had caught him in perfect light, the dust around him transformed into a halo.

Little Legion was beautiful, no doubt. Even as a grown man, he still possesses all of this beauty. But the photograph, envisioned by Eleanor Ashby's masterful eye, turned little Legion Kane into something... ethereal.

Something... supernaturally splendid.

Something... *alluring*.

And I know that's the wrong word—it's so fucking wrong—but it's true. This perfect child drowning in golden light evokes an almost uncontrollable desire to... *possess*.

Even then, looking at a photograph that was nearly two decades old, I wanted to scoop him up out of that picture and hug him tight.

Every picture gave off that same feeling. That same gut-wrenching desire to... have him. Hold him. Keep him.

That's why I didn't stop. That's why I kept turning pages. I needed to see them all. Every single one.

The pull was something like an addiction.

Closing that book and walking away, I felt like a junkie craving a fix even though there was a lot in there that made me sick.

The ones of us together.

All those stolen moments I thought were private—kissing behind hay bales, my fingers in his hair, his hands feeling up places they shouldn't have. Mother had seen it all. Documented it all.

And the later pages. Studio portraits. Professional lighting. Legion, half-dressed or barely covered at all, posed like a model but looking like a sacrifice. The light catching on shoulder blades that were already inked up, the beginning of the story of the demons inside him.

I still don't know why he did it.

I have no idea what she wanted from him.

It was the final photo that broke me.

Eleanor and Legion together in an Ashby truck. Windows down, summer heat. A selfie, of all things. She looked radiant at forty-eight.

He looked... *comfortable* beside her.

Like they were friends.

Standing here on this porch, with Colt's Range Rover disappearing into dust, I finally understand. The rot in my family goes deeper than Cash's anger or Wyatt's drinking. It's not just snobbery or social climbing.

My mother's obsession with Legion wasn't so different from what Colt did to Destiny. Different ages, different methods, but the same corruption wearing the mask of benevolence.

The Ashbys don't preserve legacy—we devour innocence and call it art.

We seduce vulnerability and call it charity.

I look down at my weeping wrist, the words "PROPERTY OF DEMON" declaring me owned when I've never felt more lost.

The Book of Legion sits in that safe still.

Waiting.

Evidence of a sickness I never named until now.

I walk through the clubhouse like I'm sleepwalking, touching walls to stay upright. My fingertips brush against concrete blocks painted black a hundred years ago, the paint gone tacky from cigarette smoke and spilled whiskey. Men's voices drop to whispers as I pass.

"Legion?" I ask, but the word just hangs there.

Nobody answers. Nobody meets my eyes.

I go upstairs to the hallway of rooms they call the bunkhouse, the steps creak under my new-to-me boots.

The narrow hallway stretches before me, ten doors on each side. Like a motel where nobody ever changes the sheets. Lightbulbs hang naked from the ceiling, casting yellow pools every few feet, leaving darkness between. The floor is bare wood, worn to splinters in the center from decades of heavy boots.

Legion and I stay in room 3. My new tattoo throbs with my pulse.

Even though we slept in here for a few hours last night, it was dark and I didn't really look at it.

Now, I do.

The room is... nothing. A twin bed, messy because I was pulled out of here early by Mama Jo this morning for the gifting. A metal footlocker, locked. No photographs, no decorations. The single window has duct tape patching a crack in the corner. Below it sits a plastic milk crate holding three books—a Bible, something with a black cover, and what looks like a Harley manual.

The room feels like a cell. Not a home. Just somewhere to lay down between fights.

I blow out a breath and leave the way I came.

Alone.

Downstairs, whispers gather around me like flies.

I step into the dining room and everything stops—conversations, coffee cups mid-lift, cigarettes hovering. Five women frozen in their places around a scarred wooden table.

Their eyes move over me in waves—down to my bleeding wrist, up to my face, across to the door like they're expecting someone else. Someone more important.

"Have any of you seen Legion?" I ask, voice steadier than I feel. I push my shoulders back like Eleanor taught me for photographs. Chin up. Smile with your eyes. Never let them see you sweat.

"He walked right past you," Brandy says, eyes sliding over to gauge my reaction.

"That doesn't answer my question," I say, sharper now. "Have you seen him, or haven't you?"

The women exchange looks loaded with meanings I can't translate. Secret language of the claimed.

I don't belong here among these women with their leather, and denim, and cigarettes. I don't belong at the ranch with its chandeliers, and silver trays, and campaign donors. I exist in the cracks between worlds now, carrying too much of both to fit in either.

But there was a vote. Thirty-nine to eight.

I might not belong, but I'm *allowed* to be here.

"If you see him," I say to the silence, "tell him I'm looking."

I turn to walk out. And almost smack right into Mama Jo.

She materializes in the doorway like she's been summoned by my defiance, silver hair pulled back in a tight braid, eyes narrowed to slits. The whispers die instantly—not fading but slaughtered. The room goes cemetery-still.

"I've got something you should see, Not Mine." Her voice carries no warmth. No invitation. Just fact.

In her weathered hand is a black burner phone, the kind they sell at gas stations for cash. The screen is scratched, the plastic case worn smooth at the edges. She extends it toward me without explanation, like I should already understand.

"Take it," she says when I hesitate.

The phone feels unexpectedly heavy in my palm. Ancient technology compared to my usual sleek devices. When I snap the cover open, the screen flickers to life, already showing a website I don't recognize.

And there I am.

Naked. On my knees on the floor of the clubhouse, leaning over Legion's lap, his fat cock in my mouth.

My breath catches, but my face stays perfectly still. Eleanor's training wins again. I scroll methodically, my thumb moving with practiced precision despite the tremor building inside my chest.

The images are explicit. Unfiltered. Raw.

Me with my lips stretched around him, looking up with hunger in my eyes. Legion's hand in my hair. My breasts exposed.

Me straddling him on that broken couch, his hands gripping my ass, my head thrown back as he thrusts inside me.

The timestamps show they were posted three hours ago. The angles suggest cameras I never saw—one high in a corner, another low and to the side. Professional setup. Not phone snapshots.

I keep scrolling, face betraying nothing while my mind catalogs every detail. The website name. The user who posted them. The comment count already climbing into the thousands.

"They're everywhere," Mama Jo says flatly. "Twitter. Reddit. The porn sites."

My entire life, captured without permission. First by my mother's artistic lens, creating the perfect childhood that never existed. Then by Marcus's social media team, crafting the perfect political wife.

Now this—my claiming, my choice, my one honest moment—stolen and distributed for strangers to consume.

Inside, something ancient and feral is clawing at my

ribs, but on the outside, I'm still Savannah Ashby, perfect in all circumstances.

My cheeks should burn with shame, but they don't. I just feel... empty. Like I've been hollowed out by the endless performance of my life.

"And?" I hand the phone back to Mama Jo.

The kitchen falls silent. Five women watching me like I might shatter.

"And?" Brandy echoes, incredulous. "You're fucking famous. These are everywhere."

I smooth my hands down the front of my borrowed jeans. "I've been famous since I was three years old. My mother sold my childhood for followers. Marcus sold my image for votes." I touch my new tattoo, the raw letters spelling PROPERTY OF DEMON. "Why should I care anymore? Why should it bother me?" The words come out calm, almost peaceful. They taste like truth—the first real truth I've spoken in years.

"Where were you three hours ago, Brandy?" Mama Jo says, suspicion hardening her features as she turns toward Brandy.

Brandy's smug smile falters. "Don't look at me. I don't have access to the security feeds."

"You think I don't see you? Creeping around, trying to matter?" Mama Jo's voice is low, dangerous. Not the practiced calm of my mother's disappointment, but something wilder. Protective without possession. "This girl just got here, and you're already trying to burn her house down."

Brandy glances at me, waiting for tears or rage, finding neither. Her certainty cracks. "I didn't leak shit."

"Then who did?" Mama Jo demands.

I laugh softly. "Who cares? Does it matter?"

Mama Jo's face hardens. "Of course it matters. This is about Badlands, not just you."

I don't say anything back. I have nothing to say.

Mama Jo studies me for a long moment, then shakes her head like she doesn't understand me. "I'm taking this to Diesel. This is club business now." She moves toward the door, pausing beside me. "You know perfectly well this matters. Your mother would've had a crisis team on the phone."

"My mother would've been more worried about the lighting than my consent," I snap back.

Some of the women exhale. They make big eyes in my peripheral vision. They snicker.

Mama Jo leaves. And, like magic, the dining room empties quickly.

No one wants to be near the fallout.

I stand alone in the silence, feeling oddly weightless.

What's done is done. The photos are out there. The perfect Savannah Ashby is dead.

And somehow, I'm still breathing.

I need to find Legion.

I need to tell him I've finally chosen my side.

CHAPTER 3
LEGION

I move through the clubhouse like I'm already dead. Eyes slide past me, conversations die, and I keep walking. No one speaks. No one touches.

Outside, the sun cuts low across the compound. The whole world laid bare from this vantage point—the Yellowstone River winding like an artery through the valley floor, Terry, Montana, the closest town, is a sad cluster of buildings looking like toys someone forgot to put away.

The Terry Badlands unfurl beyond like a violent dream, their twisted rock spires and clay formations rising from the earth like ancient bones. Wind and water have carved this landscape into something unnatural—ridges sharp as knife wounds, valleys deep as regrets, colors bleeding from rust-red to bone-white under the merciless sun. A terrain that's been tortured by time and elements, sculpted by pain into something both beautiful and wrong.

Something deep in my chest cavity vibrates in

recognition, like my body knows its twin when it sees it. This land and me, we're made of the same broken stuff.

And this high up, I can see everything that matters and nothing I need.

I keep walking. My boots drag gravel with each step. The compound spreads around me—cinderblock buildings, chain-link fences topped with razor wire, outbuildings that started as storage and became whatever was needed. Ratchet's garage. The armory. The laundry room.

I pass the laundry building and notice a stack of spiral notebooks on the front desk. Small ones, pocket-sized. The kind you can hide. The kind that holds secrets.

I take one. And a pen. Both disappear into my pocket.

The brand on my chest throbs with each heartbeat. Infection or belonging, I can't tell the difference anymore.

Mercy. I need to find Mercy.

The guilt sits like lead in my stomach. I should have gone to her first after the vote. Before the drinks, and the dancing, and the tattooing. Before Colt. Before Destiny. Before the gun and the baby and the choice I had to make for the sake of the club, for Savannah, for my sanity...

I head toward the playground—a sad collection of rusted equipment where clubhouse kids sometimes hang out. It's where Mercy's been spending her days while I've been busy trying to keep us all alive.

She's there. But she's not alone.

Two boys. Twelve, maybe thirteen. Circling her like they're playing some game, but I know that look. I wore that look once, watching Savannah from across the church playground when we were kids. Before I knew what hunger was.

These boys are too young to understand the thing growing in them. But I'm not.

Fury bubbles up from somewhere deep and dark. Three days. I looked away for three fucking days, and already they're circling her. The world doesn't wait. It doesn't forgive. It doesn't give little girls time to be little girls.

Destiny's face flashes in my mind. Fourteen and nothing but hard edges remaining of her childhood. Seventeen and pregnant. Eighteen and someone else's.

I failed her. I let her slip through my fingers while I was inside, paying for crimes that weren't mine, thinking I was protecting her by staying silent.

And now she's gone. With a baby that has Ashby eyes.

Never again.

I make a vow right there, standing in the dirt with the sun at my back and the taste of metal in my mouth. Mercy will not suffer the same fate. She will not be another Kane girl broken by men who take what isn't theirs to take.

I will burn this whole fucking world to the ground before I let that happen.

I whistle, sharp and low.

Mercy's head snaps up. She sees me. She knows that sound.

I get a hold of my anger before she reaches me,

forcing a smile. Not my real one—the one that says I'm fine when I'm not. The one that doesn't scare children.

She smiles back, but it's thin. Careful. Too much like mine.

"Whacha doin'?" I ask. Trying to be casual.

Mercy narrows her eyes. "Talkin'. Why?"

The boys hover at the edge of the playground, uncertain now that I'm here.

"This is not a place for girls."

"You already told me that. And then you disappeared for three days."

Her words *land*. Three days. Seventy-two hours of her waiting, wondering if I was coming back. Just like before. Just like always.

"I didn't disappear—I..." But I don't wanna tell her what happened. I don't wanna tell her that Destiny was here, either. That the baby was born. That her name is Marigold. That I love that name and I love my sisters too.

But I failed them both. One's gone. One's standing in front of me with eyes too old for her face.

"You what?" she pushes, and there's an edge to her voice that I'm not used to. "You got caught with Savannah." She crosses her arms over her chest. "I already know."

I crouch down to her level, my knees cracking. My ribs scream where Cash's boot connected. "It's complicated, Mercy."

"Everything with you is complicated, *Legion*." She kicks at the dirt as she sneers my name, sending a cloud of dust over my boots. "Those boys said their dads are mad at you. They said you brought trouble here."

I glance at the boys, who are pretending not to listen while obviously straining to hear every word. One belongs to Roach, I think. The other might be Ledger's nephew.

"Those boys need to mind their own business," I say, loud enough for them to hear.

"Is she your girlfriend now?" Mercy asks, her voice small. "She got a tattoo of your name on her wrist. Demon. Not Legion, *Demon*."

I don't know how to answer that. Savannah is… everything.

And nothing I can explain to a nine-year-old.

"She's important to me," I say finally. "And she's staying with us for a while."

"In our house?"

"No. Here. At the clubhouse."

Mercy's face clouds. "So we're staying here too?"

I wanna say no. I wanna say, well… just no. But there's nothing I can do right now. Half a night of refuge isn't enough time to burn off the heat of what happened.

"Yeah," I breathe. "We're staying. But Mercy, you cannot hang around those boys. They're too…" *Much like me, I don't say…* "They're too…"

Mercy scoffs. "I'm not Destiny."

"No," I agree. Unsure of exactly what she means by that. I don't even wanna think about what she might mean by that. Nine-year-old girls should not compare themselves to their knocked-up teenage sisters and decide to be the opposite.

I blow out a breath. "Can you just trust me? I mean, I get it. There's really no kids here. They're probably all you've got. But you can't have them, Mercy. Ya just can't."

Her mouth is a flat line of anger. "Then who the hell am I supposed to talk to."

I point at her for the swearing. "Me. You talk to me. "

"You're busy. And don't say Savannah. She's busy too. I'm not even allowed to go inside the clubhouse no more. If I do, then Mama Jo is gonna take away 'my privileges'." She makes little air quotes for those last two words. "Whatever the hell that means, because from the way I see it, the hot-dog dinners and tortilla-and-beans breakfast aren't what I'd call a privilege."

My laugh is so unexpected, it comes out loud. "No. I guess they aren't. But... what Mama Jo is really saying—"

"Don't over-explain things to me, Legion. I know what she's saying. This isn't a place for girls. But I'm a girl. So what am I supposed to do?"

It's a good question. I grab her by the shirt and pull her along after me.

She balks, but I don't let go. I take her over to the laundry room where someone's woman is apparently in charge.

"Hi," I say. Flashin' her a charming smile. "I'm Legion, I don't think we've met."

She smiles back. I have that effect on people—especially women. "I'm Giselle."

"Are you..."

"No. I'm not a hang-around. I'm Dusty's regular girl."

I don't even know who Dusty is. One of the prospects, probably. But it doesn't matter. If she's not a whore, I'm good. "This is my sister, Mercy. She needs a job."

Giselle, being a clubhouse woman, gets my meaning. She studies Mercy, pretendin' to look her over with a critical eye. "Well," Giselle says. "I don't hire just any old girl for the laundry. It's a good job."

Mercy makes a face, and with it comes another scoff. "What's so special about laundry?"

"It's air conditioned," Giselle says smoothly. "And no one comes out here. You know what I do all day, Mercy?"

"Laundry?"

"Well, of course, I do laundry. If I didn't, people would complain and I wouldn't have this cool job no more. But that's easy. What I really do is listen to audiobooks."

"Audiobooks?" Mercy is interested in this perk. "What kind of audiobooks."

Please, I pray. *Please do not say dark romance. Please, please—*

"Mysteries."

"Thank fuck," I blurt.

"Yeah," Giselle continues. "And, if I let you work here in my AC with my cool audiobooks going all day, that would be a privilege."

Mercy side eyes me.

I shake my head and put up my hands. "I did not tell her to say that."

"Hundreds of girls have asked to work with me in the laundry, Mercy. I've turned them all away because they didn't wanna work. They just wanted my AC and audiobooks. So…"

"I'd work," Mercy says. "Laundry's easy. I've been doing my own laundry since I was six."

Six. Three years. The guilt never stops.

"Well." Giselle looks at me. "Can you confirm this, Legion?"

"I can. She's real good at laundry."

Giselle folds her arms. "OK. But you're on probation. One week. If I catch you being lazy, I'll have to fire you."

Mercy lets out a long breath, steals a look back over her shoulder at the boys—still hovering, those sons-of-fuckin'-bitches—and relents. "I'll work. I like AC. And I've never listened to an audiobook."

Giselle guides her inside, talkin' about whatever the hell is on the audiobook menu today. When she takes one final look over her shoulder at me, I mouth the words, *"Thank you."* She gives me a small nod, then turns her attention back to her mini-employee.

Satisfied, I cross the compound. Headin' north where the buildings thin out and the scrub takes over. The old hunting blind sits crooked on stilts against the skyline—abandoned since they built the new watchtower. Back when I first started running with Badlands, I'd come out here when the noise got to be too much. When I needed to breathe without someone watching.

The ladder creaks under my weight, but the trap door swings open easy with a push of my palm, and I haul myself into the blind.

Someone's been here. Not recently, but enough to leave traces. Blankets folded in the corner. A camp stove, tarnished from weather. Coffee pot. Can of off-brand coffee. Two tin cups.

I stand in the center, suddenly feelin' like I'm trespassing in someone else's sanctuary. The thought twists something in my chest.

That's the thing no one tells you about gettin' out. Life goes on without you. The world doesn't pause while you're payin' your debt. For three years I sat inside Whitefall, fightin' through each day, taking my beatings, earning my place in the hierarchy. Six days in the Pit taught me more about silence than the twenty-nine years that came before it.

And all that time, what did I think about? Myself. Like the fucking universe orbited around Legion Kane and his pain. Like my absence left a hole nobody could fill.

But the truth is, everyone's just tryin' to survive. Even the wolves. Even the men who think they're kings. We're all just animals scratchin' for territory, for food, for somewhere safe to lick our wounds.

Very little inside Badlands counts as private property. The office belongs to Brick. Sacred ground. Everything else is communal—claimed by whoever needs it most in the moment.

Right now, that's me.

I pick up one of the blankets and drop it down next to the wall. Then I lower myself to the floor, back against the particle board wall where I can see both the compound and the distant hills, and pull out the little spiral notebook and the pen.

For a moment, I'm back in Whitefall. Back in my cell with nothing but concrete walls and these little spiral notebooks I'd buy from commissary. Writing was something I did on the inside, and I did it on the regular. So regular, I had dozens of these little fucking spiral notebooks by the time it was all said and done. I filled every single one of them up—tiny, cramped writing covering every inch of paper.

The guards would take them during contraband checks sometimes. But they never gave them back. Probably sold them to the feds thinking I was stupid enough to write down club business or confessions.

But there was never anything about Badlands in there. Nothing about deals, or names, or territory.

Just... thoughts. Questions. The kind of shit that keeps you awake when you're alone with nothing but your heartbeat for company.

I didn't write about me. Didn't write about my time. Didn't write about the other guys, or crime.

I wrote about life, and the lessons learned. Just tryin' to make sense of why this place even exists.

Why.

Why.

Why?

I click the pen. Unclick it. Click it again.

Then I open the spiral notebook to the first blank page and start to write…

Life don't hand out answers, it just keeps throwing shit at the wall to see what breaks first. Maybe it's your body, maybe it's your will, maybe it's your damn sense of what's fair. People talk like there's meaning tucked somewhere deep in the grind, like if you suffer long enough you earn some kind of prize. But all I ever saw was pain stacking up on pain, like bricks in a wall you end up building around yourself just to breathe.

Maybe the point isn't to break out. Maybe it's to learn the shape of the cell. Figure out who you are when no one's watching, when there's no applause, no woman in your bed, no gun in your hand, just you and the dark, and the quiet, and the question you keep asking even though you already know the answer: what the hell am I doing this for?

CHAPTER 4
SAVANNAH

I wander the clubhouse, looking for Legion. But apparently, he's a ghost. Because he's definitely not here. Inside the bar it's just Brandy, and Lord help me, if I have to talk about those pictures right now I might actually scream.

"Have you seen Legion?"

That's all I say. That's all I care about.

But of course she turns around with her whole face braced for war. "It wasn't me."

I blink. "What?"

"The videos. Everyone's saying I leaked 'em." She sets down a bottle. "I didn't. I'd never do that to the club."

I let out a breath and wave a hand because no. Just… no. "I don't care, Brandy." I mean it. "Have you seen Legion or not?"

"Nope." Then she turns back around like we never spoke.

And that's it. That's the end of that conversation.

I continue my aimless searching and find myself in a hallway I've never seen before, which, honestly, could describe this whole damn place.

The doors don't have signs. The lights flicker like they're just as tired as I am. And of course I have no idea where I came from. Directionally challenged in an outlaw compound. Super smart.

But whatever. I'll grid search the place if I have to. Room by room. Building by building. How hard can it be to find one six-foot-two tattooed man in a place where everyone is six-foot-something and tattooed?

When I come to a door, I push it open without knocking. The room is bright, sterile. Chains is hunched over someone's arm, needle buzzing like a fly trapped in a jar. He doesn't look up. Doesn't even pause.

There's a woman sitting near the wall. She sees me. Immediately. Like she was waiting for me to walk in.

And yeah—I remember her. The ceremony. The bullet.

"Thanks," I say, fingers brushing the necklace she gave me like it means something. Like I've figured it out.

She shrugs. "Time to let go."

Cool. Vague wisdom from the woman with the haunted eyes. Great.

"I'm Savannah," I say, because I don't know what else to do. "You know that already, but—"

"You want my name."

"Well, that's usually how it works."

She almost smiles. Not quite. "Haven't seen him."

Flat. Final. No curiosity. No warmth. The needle buzzes. Chains doesn't react.

I keep going anyway. "He's not in the clubhouse."

She shifts. Just slightly. Looks down at the ink. Watches the machine instead of me.

And I get it. That's the answer.

I turn to go.

But then—behind me—"Lita."

That's all she says. Just the name. No explanation. No tone.

That's all I get. But I smile anyway.

Not for her. For me.

Because I walked into that room still hoping someone might help. And I'm not making that mistake twice.

Outside, I let out a breath as I walk, wondering where else I could look. My new-to-me boots crunch on the gravel as I head toward the row of buildings near the fence line, no real plan in mind. Just walking like I've got somewhere to be. It's either that or stand still and look confused, and I'm not handing that win to anyone.

One of the doors up ahead stands out—heavy, reinforced. I walk up to it, curious, and come face to face with a guy with a shaved head, the woman who gave me the handkerchief, and the very specific smell of gun oil and steel.

The man is sorting magazines into crates with the kind of precision I've only seen in military movies. His hands move with automated efficiency, like he's done this ten thousand times.

The handkerchief woman stands beside him, pen

scratching across a clipboard. She's checking things off a list, murmuring numbers that the man confirms with single-syllable grunts.

These two people are a lesson in contradictions, a study in contrasts that makes me wonder how they even inhabit the same universe, let alone the same relationship.

The woman's got this vintage thing going—cardigan, manicured hands, fresh, clean-girl face. Meanwhile the guy looks like he was forged in a machine shop and never came out. It shouldn't make sense. But somehow it does. Like a Sunday picnic where the potato salad is laced with C4.

I wait at the threshold for a beat, not wanting to startle anyone in the vicinity of automatic weapons. The woman notices me first. She smiles—an actual smile with actual warmth. It's so unexpected I almost take a step back.

"Excuse me," I say, using my polite voice. "I'm looking for Legion."

The man doesn't look up. "No."

That's it. Just... no. No inflection. No eye contact. Nothing.

The woman beside him sighs and puts down her clipboard. "Don't mind Havoc. He's just focused. I'm June."

She doesn't look anything like the other women here. No leather, no hard edges. She looks... house-wife-y. Like she wandered into the wrong building.

"Savannah," I say, though she obviously knows that.

"We haven't seen Legion," June says, tucking a strand of honey-blonde hair behind her ear. "But Havoc and I were just talking and we decided that the two of you should come to dinner tonight. Our place isn't far. The kids would love to meet you."

The man, Havoc, apparently, straightens up—all six-foot-whatever of him—and stares at me. Doesn't say anything. Just looks.

I feel my throat go dry. There's something in his gaze—not hostile, exactly. More like he's measuring me for a coffin.

"I'd love to," I say, plastering on my best Ashby smile. The kind of yes I was raised to give, even when I have no idea what I was agreeing to.

June beams. "Wonderful! Havoc makes the best ribs you've ever tasted."

I nod, backing toward the door. I need to find Legion before I accidentally commit to any more social engagements with people who could probably kill me seventeen different ways.

As I turn to leave, Havoc calls, "Dinner's at seven sharp." His voice is low and mean. "Tell Legion if my kids can be at the table on time, so can he."

I smile again—practiced for just such an occasion. Fish-out-of-water meets man-who-could-disappear-me-and-still-make-it-home-for-bedtime-stories. And then quickly leave.

Outside, the sound of gunfire cuts through the air. Not random shots but a controlled rhythm—three quick bursts, then silence, then three more. I follow it like a beacon.

The shooting range sits at the edge of the property, half-hidden behind a row of shrubs. It's crude but functional—a dirt berm, paper targets pinned to metal stands, brass casings scattered across packed earth.

Two young men stand side by side, firing at human-shaped targets. They look younger than the rest of the men I've interacted with so far. A larger man stands behind them, arms crossed over his chest like a disappointed father.

There's not a single woman here. No buffer, no translator between worlds. Just men with guns.

I hesitate at the edge of the range, feeling the weight of the man's gaze shift to me. He doesn't smile, or nod, or acknowledge me in any way. Just watches, waiting to see what I'll do.

But on his vest—cut, whatever they call it—is a handy little name-tag patch. Butch, it reads.

Feeling stupidly brave, I step directly into Butch's line of sight, close enough that he can't ignore me, but far enough that I'm not interfering with whatever lesson he's teaching.

"Excuse me," I say, my voice steady despite the guns. "I'm looking for Legion."

Butch's face remains impassive. He's older—fifty maybe, with lines carved deep around his eyes. His arms stay crossed, fingers tapping against his bicep like he's counting something only he can hear.

"Haven't seen him," he says, finally. His voice is surprisingly quiet, forcing me to lean in slightly to hear him over the ringing in my ears from the gunfire.

I start to turn away when he speaks again.

"You wearing that ink or is it wearing you?"

I stop, my hand instinctively covering the scabbing on my wrist.

"You're not the first pretty girl to get a man's name put on her skin," he continues. "Won't be the last. Question is—you get it because you want everyone to know who you belong to, or because you're trying to convince yourself?"

The younger men have stopped firing, pretending to reload while they eavesdrop. I don't say anything back to Butch. Mostly because his question was quite deep and layered and I'm not sure how to answer.

Which, now that I think about it, was probably the point.

Butch holds my gaze for three more seconds, then nods once and turns back to his students.

"Again," he tells them. "And this time, breathe through it."

I walk away, the sound of renewed gunfire following me across the compound.

I head toward the garage next—a massive steel building with its bay doors thrown open. The noise hits me before I even cross the threshold: metal on metal, engines revving, air compressors hissing.

Inside, the space is cavernous. Motorcycles in various states of repair line the concrete floor. Some are gleaming beasts ready for the road, others just skeletons of metal and parts. The air smells like gasoline and something else—something metallic and masculine that smells distinctly of men.

Unlike the bar or the shooting range, this place feels alive. Men move with purpose, calling to each other over the din, passing tools back and forth. It reminds me of the ranch when we're preparing for a cattle drive

—that same focused energy, that same invisible choreography.

Six men notice me immediately, heads turning in sequence like dominoes falling. The conversations don't stop completely, but they quiet, words tapering off mid-sentence.

The nearest man is wearing worn jeans and work boots caked with grease and dirt. The denim around the ankles is so saturated with oil it looks black. He looks at me as I approach, his expression blank. His face is smeared with grease and his dark hair is pulled back into a long braid.

"Hello…" I read the name-tag patch on his cut. "Ratchet." Feeling a tiny bit smug that I've come up with a cheat sheet. It's like placards at a formal dinner. "I'm looking for Legion. Have you seen him?"

Ratchet wipes his hand on his thigh, leaving a fresh streak of black. His eyes move over me deliberately, from my borrowed boots, to my borrowed jacket, to my scabbing wrist. It's not a sexual assessment—it's mechanical. Like he's trying to identify make and model, checking for recalls or defects.

"Haven't seen him," he says finally, and there's no hostility in it. Just fact.

I glance behind me, feeling the weight of eyes. The other mechanics have resumed their work, but they're watching. Not staring, not leering, just… observing. There's nothing sharp in their attention, no judgment or threat. But no warmth either.

Just curiosity. Like I'm a new part waiting to prove it fits.

"If you do see him," I say, "tell him I'm looking for him."

Ratchet nods once, then slides back into his work without another word.

I wander for a few minutes. Just looking around the dusty compound, hoping for a glimpse of the man I love. And I'm about to give up and go back to the room and wait him out, when I catch a whiff of something different—fabric softener and soap cutting through the diesel and dust.

Following my nose, I round the corner of another building and spot a squat cinderblock structure with steam puffing from vents along the ground.

The laundry room.

Looking through the windows I see industrial washers thumping against the concrete floors and massive dryers rumbling with heat.

I let out a breath, because even though I didn't do my own laundry growing up, it's something I understand.

It's also a jackpot. Because Mercy is here, standing beside a folding table, her small hands smoothing wrinkles from a stack of white towels. Next to her is the woman who gave me the denim jacket I'm wearing now.

When I open the door, the air is immediately thick with humidity, cooled with blasting AC, and it smells like clean cotton.

"Savannah!" Mercy's face lights up when she sees

me, and it's the first genuinely happy reaction I've gotten since I started this search.

"Hey," I say, stepping inside. The door swings shut behind me, muffling the compound noise. AC washes over me like falling snow. "You work here now?"

Mercy nods proudly. "I'm the official towel folder. And I get to listen to audiobooks." She points to a small speaker on the shelf. "We just finished a mystery where the Bonekiller Murderer was caught by the fresh-faced FBI agent. Next, we're gonna listen to Harry Potter."

The woman in charge glances up from her folding. Her eyes linger on my jacket, and I suddenly feel self-conscious.

"Thank you again," I say, touching the denim. "For the jacket. I didn't have a chance to tell you earlier. I didn't really understand what was happening."

She waves me off. "It was in lost and found for months. No big deal. I'm Giselle, by the way. Dusty's woman."

"Nice to meet you. I'm looking for Legion. Have either of you seen him?"

Mercy's says, "He dropped me off here like an hour ago. Then he walked that way." She points toward the eastern edge of the compound.

"Toward the old fence line?" Giselle asks, and Mercy nods.

Giselle turns to me. "There's an old hunting blind out that way. People go there sometimes." She pauses, selecting her words carefully. "For privacy."

"A hunting blind?" I repeat.

Giselle nods. "Follow the dirt path past the shooting

range. When you hit the fence with the broken top, look left. You'll see it."

"Thank you," I say, feeling a rush of relief. Finally, a real lead after wandering this compound for what feels like hours.

"Put in a good word for me," Mercy calls as I turn to leave.

I smile at her, this small fierce girl folding towels in a biker compound laundry room. "I will."

I push back into the sunlight, orienting myself toward the eastern edge of the property. Hopeful that my endless wandering will come to an end soon.

CHAPTER 5
LEGION

They call them demons like they don't wear wings too; like fire isn't holy if it comes from below; like a man with a trigger and no prayers left doesn't count as a god if he stands alone.

But I've seen angels with blood-stained knuckles and demons who weep for the innocent. I've walked in silence where darkness swallows time, where men become ghosts before they die.

The world divides everything neat—heaven above, hell below—but the truth bleeds across those lines.

I've learned that salvation isn't coming. Not for sinners who wear their crimes like armor. Not for men who love what they can't have because of who they are.

This is the space between—not fallen, not risen.

Just standing.

Just breathing.

Just waiting for judgment that never comes because I already carved it into my own flesh and—

"Legion!"

My pen stops mid-sentence as Savannah's voice calls

up from below. I'd forgotten about her. I crawl across the plywood floor, careful of the weak spots where the rain's gotten in over the years. The trapdoor creaks when I pull it open, sending down a shower of dust and splinters.

And there she is, looking up at me. Savannah Ashby with her blonde hair catching the late afternoon sun, making a halo like she's part hallucination, part fantasy. Her face is tilted up, eyes squinting against the light. There's something different about her now—something wild and uncertain I never saw before prison.

"What are you doing up there?" Savannah calls, her hand shielding her eyes.

"Just thinking." I push the trapdoor wider. "Needed some quiet."

Her fresh tattoo catches the light—PROPERTY OF DEMON—still red around the edges. My chest tightens at the sight. It wasn't supposed to be like this. She wasn't supposed to end up here, marked by my world.

I slide the notebook under the blanket beside me, tucking it away like a secret. "Come on up. Ladder's old but it'll hold."

She tests the first rung with her boot—the boots someone gave her to replace her bare feet. Everything she's wearing belongs to someone else now. "I've been looking for you everywhere," she says, voice strained with the effort of climbing. "Nobody knew where you were."

"That's because I'm a stranger here these days."

Savannah is about half way up when this comes out. She stops, looking at me with squinting eyes. "What?"

I laugh. It's real, too. Because the writing did the

trick. It put the demon away after Colt let him out. "Nothin'," I say. "Come on. It's nice up here."

The ladder creaks under her weight, and I reach down to grab her wrist when she's close enough, pulling her up the last few rungs. Her skin is warm against mine, pulse fluttering under my thumb.

For a second, we just stare at each other. Her face is still haunted by what Marcus did to her for three days.

"Found me," I sigh, letting go of her wrist.

She looks around the blind—at the blankets piled in the corner, the camp stove, the tin cups. "What's goin' on up here?"

"Just… thinkin'," I say, moving back to sit against the wall. "It's a nice quiet little place to do that."

"I've been looking for you," she says, crawling over to me. I open my legs up and she settles between them, collapsing against my chest, like we've been doing this every day, all our lives. Immediately, my fingers find her hair and start playing with it.

"After everything with Colt and—"

"Don't." The word comes out harder than I meant it to. "I don't wanna talk about that."

"All right." She doesn't argue.

Then I feel like an ass, so have the urge to explain. "It's just… it's not even Colt, ya know?"

Savannah sits up a bit, trying to look at me. "How could it not be about Colt? He's thirty-one years old. She's seventeen. Eighteen now, but…"

She sighs.

I sigh.

"Yeah. He's…" I blow out a breath. "I dunno. She

could do worse, I guess. She could've ended up here, ya know?"

"Hmmm." This hum of hers says a whole lot without sayin' anything at all.

It says... *I* ended up here.

It says... *you* brought me here.

It says... *you failed*.

"There are pictures of us all over the internet," Savannah says. "Someone leaked videos of last night."

"For fuck's sake. *Who*?"

"Not sure. Mama Jo thinks it's Brandy, but she's denying it."

"I'm sorry, Savannah. I'm so fucking sorry I ever brought you here. What the hell was I thinking?" I start to get up. "We need to—"

"No," she says, pushing back on me. "Just..." she sighs. "Can we just take a breath?" She turns her body, repositioning so she can see me. "All I want is to *be* with you. I don't care where it is."

"It's all I want. Ever wanted. You're it, Savannah. You've been my dream since that first time at the silo. Before I even knew what it meant to love someone like this, I loved you."

She smiles up at me. "Whatever happens to us, as long as it's us and we're not alone, we'll be OK."

It's bullshit, these words. It's not even remotely true. But I don't want her to know that. I'll do anything to keep her from knowing that.

She leans up and kisses me. Her lips taste both sweet and salty. And it reminds me of how into it she was last night. How she took my cock in her mouth—

"Yes, what?" I ask back.

"Yes, I want you inside me right now."

I chuckle. "That's not what I was thinking."

"Not yet," she says.

For a moment, all I see in her is sadness. Loss. Betrayal. It kills me.

And she knows I can see it, because she puts a fingertip on my lips. "No. Don't think. Just… take me." These last two words aren't even a sound. Just her lips moving around the letters. "Talk dirty to me, Legion."

"Why, Savannah? When I could just talk sweet to you instead? Wouldn't you like that better?"

"If you talk sweet to me right now, it'll sound like pity. That's what you're thinking. You're… *re-thinking*. I shouldn't be here. We aren't gonna make it. The world is a cruel place and happy endings don't exist."

I don't reply, because she's right. That *is* what I'm thinking.

"I don't want you to feel sorry for me, Legion. Protect me? Sure. Rescue me when I need it? Absolutely. But all the other times, I want you to… " She looks away for a moment. Up at the water-stained ceiling like she's thinking. "I want you to take me for granted."

"What?" I almost laugh.

"Not in a bad way. Just… a for-sure way. Like you know, with one-hundred-percent certainty, that I will *always* be here." She places her hand on the side of my cheek. "Take me for granted. Talk dirty to me. Fuck me any way you want. And by doing this, you're sending a signal. A signal that says, you're so sure of my love, you assume it will be there tomorrow."

This sounds… well, crazy as all hell. The words are

hard to put together because she's trying to describe a feeling of... comfortablenesss. Not even sure that's a word, which is the problem.

She's trying to define... emotional certainty. A kind of sacred mundanity. The feeling of being so woven into someone's daily existence that your presence isn't a question—it's a given.

And I get it.

That's what I want too.

Someone who is so completely mine, I feel certain that she will be by my side no matter what.

No matter how far away, no matter how mad she is, no matter what.

We are a *we*. And we won't ever be alone again, even if we are.

Savannah gets up on her knees and takes off her jacket, throwing it across the small room. She tilts her head, smiling coyly at me.

So I help her with the shirt. Lifting it up over her head, watching as her tits appear. The moment I toss it, she starts clawing for mine. Taking off my cut, then my shirt joins hers on the floor.

For a moment, we're still. I watch her as she studies the tattoos on my chest.

Her fingertips trace the archangel's sword raised in the air, like triumph, if you don't look too hard at the defeat on his face. At the wounds in his side. Wounds he earned.

Below the angel, the demon wails. No sword in him now. That's the problem with the moment after.

The evidence is somewhere else.

"They're both dying," she whispers.

"Yeah." My voice comes out rough. "That's the point."

She leans down, presses her lips against the brand that marks me as Badlands property. The infection makes it burn, but I don't pull away. Pain and pleasure—they've always lived in the same house for me.

"I want you," she says against my skin.

I run my hand up her back, feeling the notches of her spine. She's lost weight since I went away. Three years of her life I missed. Three years of her changing while I stayed the same, locked in concrete and counting minutes.

"You sure?" I ask, even as my cock hardens against her thigh. "I mean, life is so fuckin' heavy right now—"

"I need this." Her eyes lock with mine, fierce and certain. "I need you. I want hard this time, Legion. I want to feel you. Your power. Your muscles, your strength. Claim me again. I want it."

I want it too. I want to claim her as mine every day for the rest of my life.

I lower her onto her back, allowing her to sort out her legs as I pin her wrists above her head with one hand. The blankets beneath us are rough and I don't care. I doubt she does either. I use my free hand to unbutton her jeans, tugging them down her hips. She lifts up, helping me.

"These aren't even yours," I growl.

"Nothing is anymore." She kicks them off. "Except you."

I press my mouth to her neck, teeth grazing the soft skin there. "Say it again."

"I'm yours," she breathes. "Only yours."

My hand slides between her legs, finding her already wet. I groan against her throat. "Fuck, Savannah. You're soaked."

"Been thinking about you all day," she says, her voice breaking as I circle her clit with my thumb. "About last night."

"About me fucking you in front of everyone?" I slip two fingers inside her, feeling her clench around them. "You liked that, didn't you? Everyone watching while I claimed what's mine."

Her back arches. "Yes."

I work my fingers deeper, curling them to hit that spot that makes her gasp. "Tell me what you want, princess."

"Your mouth," she moans. "Please."

I release her wrists, moving down her body. I pause at her breasts, taking each nipple into my mouth, sucking and biting until she's writhing beneath me. Then I continue lower, trailing kisses down her stomach.

When I reach the apex of her thighs, I look up at her. Her eyes are half-closed, lips parted, cheeks flushed. She's never been more beautiful than she is right now—marked by my name, desperate for my touch.

"Spread your legs wider," I command.

She obeys instantly, opening herself to me. I take a moment just to look at her, pink, and swollen, and glistening wet. Mine. All fucking mine.

I lower my head and lick a long, slow stripe up her center. She tastes like heaven—like something I was never meant to have but took anyway.

"Oh, God," she gasps, her hands flying to my hair.

I devour her like a starving man, my tongue circling her clit before dipping inside her. Her thighs tremble on either side of my head, her fingers tightening in my hair. I slip my fingers back inside her as I suck her clit, and she cries out.

"That's it," I murmur against her. "Let me hear you."

Her hips buck against my face as I increase the pressure, working my fingers in and out while my tongue flicks rapidly over her clit. She's close—I can feel it in the way she tightens around my fingers, in the pitch of her moans.

"Legion," she pants. "I'm gonna—"

"Come for me," I growl. "Now."

Her entire body goes rigid as she shatters, a broken cry tearing from her throat. I don't let up, working her through it, lapping up every drop of her release until she's pushing at my shoulders, oversensitive.

I rise up, wiping my mouth with the back of my hand. "Good girl."

She smiles at me. Coyly. Knowingly. Boldly. She reaches for my belt, fumbling with the buckle. "I need you inside me."

I help her, undoing my jeans and shoving them down just enough to free my cock. It springs up, hard and aching. I position myself at her entrance, then slide the head into her pooling wetness.

"Tell me you want this," I say, my voice strained. "Tell me you're mine."

"I want this," she says, her eyes locked on mine. "I'm yours, Legion. Only yours."

I push into her in one smooth thrust, burying myself inside her pussy. We both groan at the sensation. She's tight and hot around me, perfect in every fucking way.

"Fuck, Savannah," I hiss through gritted teeth. "You feel so good."

I start to move, setting a slow, deep rhythm. Each thrust drives me deeper into her, claiming her all over again. Her legs wrap around my waist, pulling me closer.

"Harder," she begs. "Please, Legion. Harder."

I grip her hips, lifting her slightly, and drive into her with renewed force. The sound of skin slapping against skin fills the small space, mixed with our heavy breathing and her little whimpers of pleasure.

"You like that?" I growl. "You like taking my cock like this?"

"Yes," she moans. "God, yes."

I increase the pace, fucking her hard and deep. Sweat beads on my forehead, drips down my chest. The brand burns with every movement, but I don't care. All that matters is Savannah beneath me, around me, taking everything I have to give.

"Touch yourself," I command. "I want to feel you come on my cock."

She slides her hand between us, her fingers finding her clit. The sight of her touching herself while I fuck her nearly sends me over the edge. I have to grit my teeth, focus on anything else to hold back.

"That's it," I encourage her. "Show me how you like it."

Her fingers move in tight circles, her breath coming in short gasps. I can feel her getting closer, her inner walls starting to flutter around my length.

"Legion," she moans. "I'm close."

"Look at me," I demand. "I want to see your eyes when you come."

Her gaze locks with mine, blue eyes wide and vulnerable. In that moment, I see everything—her fear, her trust, her love. It's almost too much to bear.

"Come for me, Savannah," I whisper. "Come all over my cock."

She breaks with a cry, her body arching beneath me, her pussy clenching around me in rhythmic waves. The sight of her coming undone pushes me to the edge.

"Fuck," I groan. "I'm gonna come. Where do you want it?"

"Inside," she gasps. "I want to feel you."

That's all it takes. I thrust deep one last time and explode, emptying myself inside her with a guttural moan. For a moment, the world narrows to just this—just us, connected in the most primal way possible.

I collapse on top of her, careful to brace most of my weight on my forearms. We're both breathing hard, skin slick with sweat. I press my forehead against hers, our breath mingling.

"I love you," she whispers, so quietly I almost miss it.

Instead of answering, I kiss her—deep, and slow, and thorough. I pour everything I can't say into that kiss. All the words that get stuck in my throat, all the promises I'm afraid to make.

When we finally break apart, I roll to the side, pulling her against my chest. She nestles into me, her head tucked under my chin, her hand resting over my heart.

I stroke her hair, feeling the silk of it between my fingers.

We lie like this.

Two people in love.

Forbidden love, but love all the same.

I don't deserve a woman like Savannah.

Everyone knows this.

Everyone but her…

CHAPTER 6
SAVANNAH

I'm not ready to leave this place. Not ready to face whatever's waiting for us outside. The real world can wait.

I turn over and straddle Legion's thighs, feeling the rough hair against my bare skin. His eyes widen slightly, a smile playing at the corners of his mouth.

"What are you doin'?" he laughs, his hands coming to rest on my hips. "Again?"

"Again," I whisper, leaning down to press my lips against his. "Again, and again, and again..."

His smile grows wider, and I feel something warm unfurl in my chest. This smile—not the careful, controlled one he shows the world, but this real one—it's mine. All mine.

"Close your eyes, Legion."

He hesitates for just a second before complying, thick lashes fanning against his cheeks. I pull back and slide down his body, dragging my tongue along the sweat-slicked planes of his chest and stomach, careful not to touch his raw, red brand. I trace the lines of his tattoos with my tongue, following the path of angels and demons across his torso.

His muscles jump under my touch, his breath catching when I reach the trail of hair below his navel. I position myself between his legs, my hair falling forward to brush against his thighs.

"Your turn," I whisper.

I take him in my hand, already half-hard again. He's heavy and warm against my palm as I stroke him slowly, watching his face. His jaw clenches, the tendons in his neck standing out as he fights to keep still.

"Watch me," I say, echoing his earlier command.

His eyes open, dark and hungry. I hold his gaze as I lower my head and take him into my mouth, just the tip at first. His back bucks involuntarily. I place my free hand on his hip, pressing him back down.

"Fuck," he groans, one hand coming up to tangle in my hair. "Savannah..."

I take him deeper, hollowing my cheeks as I suck. His taste is complex—salt and musk and something uniquely him. I work him with my hand and mouth together, establishing a rhythm that has him cursing under his breath.

"Tell me what you want," I say, pulling back just enough to speak. "Tell me how to make you feel good."

"Deeper," he says, his voice strained. "Take me deeper, baby."

I comply, relaxing my throat to take him as far as I can. His grip on my hair tightens, not quite painful but close—a delicious edge that makes me moan around him.

"Oh, fuck," he hisses. "Just like that. Don't stop."

I don't. I work him with everything I have, determined to make him lose control the way he always makes me lose mine. His breathing grows ragged, his thighs tensing beneath me.

"Wait," he says suddenly, tugging at my hair. "Stop."

I pull back, looking up at him in confusion. "What's wrong?"

"Nothing's wrong," he says, his chest heaving. "I just want to be inside you when I come."

He sits up and reaches for me, pulling me up his body until I'm straddling him again. I can feel him hard and hot against me, pressing against my entrance.

"Ride me," he says, his hands gripping my hips. "I want to watch you take control."

I lift myself up and position him at my entrance, then slowly sink down onto him. We both groan as he fills me completely. I brace my hands on his chest, careful to avoid the brand, and start to move.

"That's it," he encourages, his thumbs digging into my hipbones. "Fuck yourself on my cock."

The words send a jolt of heat through me. I've never been one for dirty talk—it always seemed so performative with other men. But with Legion, it feels natural. Real.

"You like that?" I ask, grinding down on him. "You like watching me fuck myself on your cock?"

He smiles at my reciprocal dirty talk. "Fuck yes," he growls. "You're so fucking beautiful like this."

I increase my pace, riding him harder. The angle lets him hit spots inside me that make my vision blur. I can feel another orgasm building, coiling tight in my belly.

I slide my hand between us, finding my clit with practiced fingers. The sensation of being filled by him while touching myself creates an almost unbearable pleasure. My body's already humming, vibrating on the edge of release.

Legion watches me with midnight eyes, his face strained with the effort of holding back. I gasp, my movements growing quicker as I continue to slide myself back and forth across his cock.

His calloused hands begin guiding my hips. Urging me on, making me fuck him faster, deeper, harder. Every thrust hits something deep inside that makes stars burst behind my eyelids. His fingers are pressing into my hips hard enough to leave marks.

But I don't care.

I like it.

I like his rough touch. I like his dirty mouth. I like the way he fucks me. I like the way he looks at me. I like the way he talks to me.

Hell, I just like him.

All of him.

And I can truly say that now that I've seen who he really is.

I am hungry for him. Starving for him.

And as I'm thinking this, I shatter completely, crying out his name as waves of pleasure crash through me like a summer storm.

Through the sweet haze of my release, I feel him thrust up hard, once, twice, his body tensing beneath mine before he follows me into oblivion with a sound that's half curse, half prayer.

I collapse onto his chest, both of us breathing hard.

His arms come around me, holding me close as the aftershocks ripple through us.

"Fuck," he says softly, pressing a kiss to my temple.

I laugh breathlessly. "Yeah."

We lie like that for a while, connected in every way possible. I trace idle patterns on arms, feeling his heartbeat gradually slow beneath my palm.

And now, I allow myself to drift...

Until I suddenly remember. "Oh, shit!"

"What?" he mumbles.

"We have dinner plans!"

He stiffens slightly beneath me. "What?"

"With Havoc and June," I explain. "At seven. She invited us when I was looking for you. I said yes, obviously."

Legion moans. His hand coming up to stroke my hair. "I don't know, Savannah. I'm not sure it's a good idea."

"Why not?"

"Because..." He pauses, seeming to search for words. "This is all happening too fast. You getting that tattoo, the vote, the leaked videos..."

I lift my head to look at him. "Are you ashamed of me?"

"What? *No*," he says immediately. "Never. I just—I don't want you getting pulled deeper into this life than you already are."

"I chose this," I remind him, touching the fresh tattoo on my wrist. It's still tender, the skin around it red and slightly swollen. "I chose *you*. And that means... playing the good little woman."

One of his eyebrows rises up to the ceiling. "Good little woman?"

"Oh, my god, Legion. Did you see that June? She's like Betty fuckin' Crocker had a baby with Jesse James."

Legion laughs. "Yeah, June is somethin' else, all right. She's military too. Her aim puts mine to shame."

"Well," I say, "I like her style. Apparently, they have kids?"

"Six," Legion deadpans.

"Six? Wow."

"Yeah." He looks at me for a long moment, his expression unreadable. Then he sighs again. "Dinner, huh?"

"Seven sharp," I say, offering him a small smile. "Havoc said if his kids can be on time, so can you."

A ghost of a smile touches his lips. "Havoc said that?"

"He did."

"Well, fuck. I guess we're having dinner with Havoc and June."

I lean down to kiss him, soft and lingering. "Thank you."

"For what?"

"For letting me in," I say. "For not pushing me away."

His expression clouds slightly, but he doesn't respond. Instead, he pulls me down for another kiss, deeper this time. I can feel him stirring against me again, his body responding to mine with a readiness that still surprises me.

"We should probably get cleaned up," I murmur against his lips.

"Probably," he agrees, but his hands are already roaming my body, tracing the curve of my spine, the flare of my hips.

"Legion," I laugh. "We'll be late."

"You're the one who started it," he says, rolling us over so I'm beneath him. "And I'm not done with you yet."

His mouth finds my breast, teeth grazing my nipple in a way that makes me arch off the blanket. All thoughts of dinner, of the outside world, vanish from my mind. There's only Legion and me and this moment, stretching out like forever.

His hands are everywhere at once—sliding down my sides, gripping my thighs, lifting my hips to meet his. Then he's workin' his way down my body with deliberate slowness, tasting every inch of me. The scratch of his stubble against my inner thighs makes me shiver, and when his mouth finally finds me, I have to bite my lip to keep from crying out.

My fingers tangle in his hair as he works me with his tongue, bringing me to the edge again and again without letting me fall. It's exquisite torture. Just when I think I can't take anymore, he slides two fingers inside me, curling them forward to hit that spot that makes me see stars.

I come apart beneath him, my body convulsing with pleasure so intense it borders on pain. But he doesn't stop. He keeps going, relentless, until I'm writhing beneath him, oversensitive and desperate.

Then he's moving up my body, positioning himself between my legs, and entering me in one smooth thrust.

The fullness, the rightness of him inside me makes me gasp.

But this time, neither of us are hard and desperate. We're soft and slow. He fucks me deep this time. His eyes never leaving mine. And as he moves within me, I have a dream. I paint pictures of a future I've never allowed myself to imagine before.

I see us in a house—not a mansion like the one I grew up in, but something real. Something ours. Maybe a renovated farmhouse with wide porches and room to breathe. Legion fixing motorcycles in a detached garage while I tend to a garden that actually grows things we eat instead of just looking pretty for Instagram.

I see children—two, three, maybe more—with his wild blond hair and my blue eyes, running through tall grass with dirty knees and fearless hearts. Legion teaching them to ride bikes and throw punches. Me teaching them to ride horses and be polite.

I see family dinners where everyone talks at once, homework spread across kitchen tables, Christmas mornings with handmade stockings hung by the fireplace. Legion reading bedtime stories in his deep voice, making all the character voices despite his protests that he's terrible at it.

I see us growing older together, watching our children become adults with their own lives, their own loves. Legion's hair going gray at the temples, laugh lines deepening around his eyes. My hands becoming more like my mother's, but gentler. Kinder.

And through it all, I see us like this—tangled together, his body moving within mine, that connection that goes beyond the physical. That thing that makes me feel like I've finally found home after a lifetime of searching.

Legion changes the angle, hitting deeper, and the fantasy dissolves as pleasure overtakes me again. He flips us over without breaking our connection, so I'm on top again. His hands guide my hips as I ride him, setting a pace that has us both gasping.

Then he's sitting up, wrapping his arms around me, holding me close as we move together. It's almost unbearably intimate—our bodies completely aligned, foreheads touching, breath mingling. I can feel him everywhere, inside and out.

When he comes, it triggers my own release, and we cling to each other through the aftershocks, neither willing to let go first.

As our breathing slows, I rest my head on his shoulder, unwilling to break the spell just yet. In this moment, that future I imagined doesn't seem so impossible. Not with him. Not if we're together.

But reality is waiting just outside this hunting blind.

Dinner with Havoc and June.

The leaked videos.

My family.

His club.

All the forces trying to pull us apart.

For now, though, I let myself believe in that farmhouse, those wild-haired children, that life where Legion and I get to be just us, without the weight of our names or our pasts.

CHAPTER 7
LEGION

Heaven is the awareness that you're not in Hell.

That's how I feel right now.

Like I'm not in Hell.

Watching Savannah in her dress that was given to her through some 'gifting' ritual that I had no idea even existed. It's a simple thing, cotton and comfortable, nothing like the designer labels she used to wear, but somehow it suits her more. Fits her like it was made for the woman she's becoming, not the one she was pretending to be.

It's nice though. That the women here have their own traditions, or whatever. For many reasons, not least of which we didn't have to go shopping for Savannah right away because she came here with nothing but the clothes on her back.

My clothes on her back, actually. Which was its own kind of heaven.

She's brushing her hair in the bathroom mirror while I watch, sitting on the bed in room 3. The mattress creaks under my weight, springs protesting like they've seen too many nights and not enough rest. The sound of the brush through her hair is hypnotic—steady, rhythmic. Makes a man think dangerous thoughts.

"What?" She asks, our eyes meeting in the mirror. There's something vulnerable in her gaze, like she's still not used to being looked at by my hungry eyes.

"Just you."

She smiles, twists her hair up into a ponytail, turns, walks over to me, and sits in my lap. Smiles again. The weight of her feels right, like the last piece of a puzzle I've been working on for years.

"Don't rev the engine if ya aren't gonna step on the gas," I warn. "Because if you get me started, I'll finish it. And that'll make us late for dinner. And just so you know, if we're late for dinner, I'll blame it on you." My hands find her hips, fingers digging in just enough to make her breath catch.

She leans in, kissing me. Someone must've given her some lip gloss because she tastes like strawberries. Sweet, and artificial, and addictive. "Later then."

"Later," I agree, smacking her ass and standing up, taking her with me. She squeals a little. But I capture that squeal in my mouth with a kiss. Her legs wrap around my waist instinctively, like her body remembers exactly how we fit together.

"Have you always been this horny? Or is this new?" I ask against her neck, as I put her down. Just breathing in the scent of her is enough to turn me on.

"What?" She smacks me on the chest, feigning offense but her eyes are dancing.

"Woman, I've fucked you like ten times in the last

twenty-four hours. I'm just wondering if I should adjust my new expectations or this is me winning the jackpot." My voice is hungry, even to my own ears.

She giggles. "I can't help it." Then she grabs my dick, right through my jeans. Her face tilts up, eyes on me, all innocence and sin mixed together. "I've never been this horny in my life. I've never been so sore, either. But if this is the price I have to pay…" She grabs me again, fingers tracing the outline with expert precision. "It's worth it."

"I'm about to turn you over my knee and spank you 'till you come for getting me all hard again," I reach down, push her hand off me, and give my junk a little shake. The denim's too tight now, uncomfortable in the best way.

She flips her hair at me. Looks at me coyly over her shoulder. "When we get home, you can spank me all you want."

Fuck's sake. I'm about to tell her we should skip dinner when she opens my door and saunters out into the hallway, leaving me behind. The sway of her hips is deliberate, a promise for later.

I guess my dick will have to wait.

But I'll make her pay for it.

In the best way possible, of course.

Outside, I strap on my helmet, watching Savannah struggle with hers. The clasp gives her trouble. I reach over, fingers brushing her throat as I snap it closed. Her pulse jumps under my touch.

"Tight enough?" I ask.

She nods, smiling at me as I get on, back up, and nod for her to get behind me. "Legs up, arms around me, lean when I lean. Don't fight the bike." The instructions I should've given her last night, but didn't, come out clipped and professional. But there's nothing professional about how my body reacts when she slides against me, thighs pressing into mine, chest against my back.

The engine growls to life beneath us, and I feel her startle, then settle. Her arms tighten around my waist, fingers locking together over my stomach. For a moment, I just sit there, letting the vibration run through both of us. Letting her get used to the way it feels to have something powerful between her legs.

Then I pick my feet up and we're moving.

Once out of the gate, the dirt road stretches out ahead, a ribbon of mottled browns and reds that cuts through the badlands landscape. Evening light bleeds across the sky, painting everything gold and crimson. When we hit the black top, I take the turns easy, feeling Savannah's body tense then relax as she follows my lead.

But once we hit the two-lane highway that will take us to Havoc's, I open it up a little. Not too much—not with her on the back. But enough to feel the wind push against us, enough to hear her gasp behind me when we crest a hill and the whole valley opens up below.

The land out here tells the truth. Nothing can hide in these broken hills. Every scar, every edge is visible for miles. Wind and water carved this place over centuries, stripping away anything soft, leaving only what's strong enough to endure.

Kinda like prison did to me.

Kinda like what Elenore did to her.

I'm more like these badlands than I like to admit. Carved out by forces I couldn't control. Weathered. Broken in places. Full of sharp edges and unexpected drops. But still standing. Still here.

We pass by many forgotten places. Places that were abandoned years ago, windows staring out like empty eye sockets. That's how it is around here—everything's temporary. When you're up against nature, nature always wins.

Once we're settled into the ride, my mind starts spinning with the words I was writing earlier. I left my notebook in the blind. I'll have to go back and get it, but like always, it doesn't say much in there.

It's just rambling. Me, doin' my best to make sense of nonsensical things. I've always been fightin' the demon. I've had that fuckin' sword in my hand since the day I was born.

But ever since Savannah came into my life when I was fourteen, the battle has breaks. Little pauses where I can—not let down my guard, that's never gonna happen—but just settle a bit.

I stop grinding and take a look around when Savannah is next to me.

I wonder what I feel like to her?

I wonder how she fights her demons?

I wonder if I'm her demon.

The turnoff to the Dun property appears, marked by

nothing but a weathered red mailbox. I slow down, taking the dirt road at a crawl to keep the dust down.

The bike's suspension protests at every rut and hole, but I navigate them carefully. Savannah's grip has relaxed a little, her body moving with mine, learning the rhythm of the road.

As we crest the final rise, the Dun place comes into view. It's nothing like the Ashby compound—no pretension, no grandeur. Just a simple white farmhouse with green shutters, a wraparound porch, and a red barn off to the side. The kind of place that says people live here, not just exist for show.

The sun catches on the tin roof, making it shine like a beacon. Around the property, life is happening everywhere you look. A fenced arena to the left holds two tiny girls on ponies, circling under the watchful eye of Havoc's oldest girl and June.

To the right, a homemade dirt track winds through a stand of cottonwoods, twin boys racing dirt bikes around it, their excited shouts carrying across the evening air.

The smell of grillin' meat hits me as I cut the engine. Havoc stands on a wooden deck off the back of the house, manning a massive grill, smoke risin' around him like he's some kind of war god overseeing a sacrifice. He's shed his cut, wearing just jeans and a faded black t-shirt, lookin' almost normal except for the gun I know is tucked into his waistband.

Savannah's arms slowly unwrap from my waist as she takes in the scene. I feel the absence immediately, like someone turned off a heater.

I swing my leg over the bike, offering her a hand to help her off.

"This is... not what I expected," she says quietly, removing her helmet, then the elastic holding her hair in the ponytail. It falls down around her shoulders, tangled from the wind.

"What were you expecting?"

"I don't know. Something more... outlawish?"

I snort. "Havoc's got a basement full of guns and probably three bodies buried out back. Don't let the picket fence fool you."

Her eyes widen, and I realize too late she can't tell if I'm joking. I'm not sure I know either.

The twin boys, maybe seven or eight, come tearing around the side of the house, dirt bikes forgotten now. They stare at Savannah like she's some exotic creature that wandered out of the woods.

"That's Legion," one whispers to the other, loud enough for us to hear. "Dad says he killed a man with his thumbs once."

"Did not," the other argues. "Dad said it was with a pencil."

Fuck's sake. I'm going to have a word with Havoc about the bedtime stories he's telling his kids.

Savannah's hand finds mine, fingers threadin' through with surprising strength. I look down at her, expecting to see fear or regret. Instead, I find something that looks almost like amusement.

"With your thumbs, huh?" she whispers.

"Apparently my reputation exceeds reality," I mutter, squeezing her hand. "You okay?"

She nods, eyes scanning the property again. "It's beautiful here," she says softly. "Peaceful."

It is. That's what makes it dangerous.

Places like this make you believe in things like normal, and safe, and forever.

They make you forget that the world is waitin' just beyond the fence line, ready to tear it all apart.

But I don't say that.

Instead, I guide her toward the house, toward Havoc and his grill and his picture-perfect family that somehow exists alongside the man who plans our gun runs and maintains our armory.

June spots us from the arena and waves, calling something to the girls before heading our way. She's all vintage cardigan and perfect ponytail, looking like she stepped out of a 1950s housewife magazine. The only thing that gives her away is the way she walks—purposeful, alert, shoulders squared. Once military, always military.

"You made it!" she calls, smile warm but eyes assessing as we wait for her to catch up. She's checking Savannah for threats, for weakness, for anything that might endanger her family. I respect that. "Dinner's almost ready. Havoc's doing his famous ribs."

"Famous for what?" I ask. "Giving people food poisoning?"

June laughs, a genuine sound that makes the kids look over. "Only that one time, and it was your own fault for eating the ones he dropped on the ground."

"He didn't tell me he dropped them."

The easy banter feels strange with Savannah watching. Two worlds colliding that were never meant to touch. But her hand is still in mine, her shoulder pressed against my arm, and she's not running. Not yet.

The twins have crept closer. And the oldest boy, the one with Havoc's serious eyes, addresses me directly. "Did you really kill someone with a pencil?"

"Finn!" June's voice snaps like a whip. "What have we told you about appropriate questions?"

"Not to ask about Dad's work or anyone's prison time," the boy recites dutifully. "But this isn't about prison, it's about a pencil."

"The only thing I've ever killed with a pencil is a math test. And I failed that too."

The boy looks disappointed but nods. The twins—identical, but mirror images—peer around me at Savannah.

"Are you his girlfriend?" one asks.

Before I can answer, Savannah says, "I'm his," showing the fresh tattoo on her wrist.

The twins' eyes go wide. "Cool," they breathe in unison.

June clears her throat. "Boys, go wash up for dinner." Then she whistles and yells in the direction of the riding arena. "Put the ponies away, girls! Dinner time now!" She turns to us with an apologetic smile. "Sorry about that. They're at an age where boundaries are... theoretical."

"It's fine," Savannah says, and I'm surprised to hear genuine warmth in her voice. "They're adorable."

"They're monsters," June corrects, but her tone is fond. "Come on, Havoc's waiting. And he hates when food gets cold."

As we follow her toward the deck, Savannah leans close to my ear. "With a pencil, really?"

"It was a pen, actually," I murmur back, then immediately regret it when her step falters. "That was a joke."

She studies my face for a long moment, then nods slowly. "No, it wasn't. But it's okay." Her fingers tighten around mine. "I'm still here."

The words hit harder than they should.

After everything—the vote, the claiming, the leaked videos, Destiny, Colt, and the baby—she's still here. Walking beside me toward a normal family dinner like we have any right to pretend we're normal too.

Havoc looks up as we approach, eyes narrowing slightly when he sees our joined hands. But he just nods, flipping a rack of ribs with practiced precision.

"Right on time," he says, which from Havoc is practically a warm welcome. "Who wants a beer?"

I guide Savannah up the steps to the deck, feeling the weight of his gaze. Havoc doesn't miss anything—not the way she leans into me, not the fresh ink on her wrist, not the hardness in her eyes that only appeared after the kidnapping.

But he doesn't comment. Just hands me a beer from the cooler at his feet, then offers one to Savannah. She hesitates, then accepts it with a small smile.

"Thank you for having us," she says, sounding for all the world like she's at one of her fancy Ashby functions instead of standing on the deck of an outlaw's family home.

Havoc grunts, turning back to his grill. "June's idea. Said you needed to see your options."

Options.

Most women who end up with bikers—especially outlaw bikers—don't have those.

But Savannah isn't most women.

She's an Ashby.

She's got plenty of fucking options.

And I'm really not sure I want her thinking too hard about them.

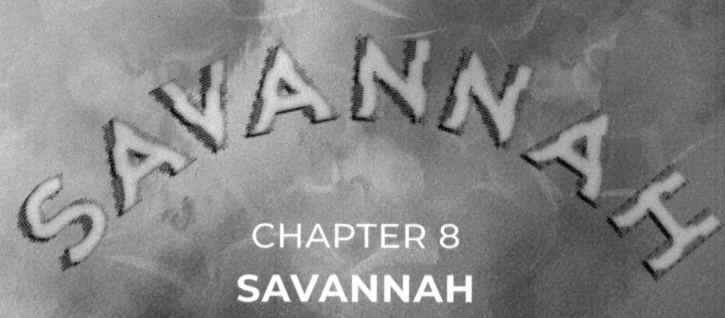

CHAPTER 8
SAVANNAH

Options.

The word hangs in the air between Legion and me. He makes a face I'm not even sure he's aware he's making. Like the word tastes bad. I lean in to him, sliding my hand across his ass and stick it into his back pocket.

He looks at me. Worried, I think. But trying not to show it.

It's easy to read his mind. Not because Legion's a simple person—he's the definition of the word complicated. But I know what people see when they look at me.

Money That's all they see is money.

Legion's not all that different. Nobody sees money when they look at him—they see… danger. Outlaw. Prison time. Maybe regrets, but then again, maybe not.

And he's much more than that. Just like I am much more than the family money I come from.

"Hey, Not Mine?" June says, interrupting my

thoughts. The nickname hits, and even Legion laughs. "Why don't you come into the house. I'll show you around and you can help me in the kitchen."

It doesn't land like a question. And when Legion gives my butt a pat, along with a kiss on the cheek, I determine it isn't.

I follow June through the front door and step into a world that looks like it was crafted specifically to make me ache with longing. The farmhouse interior is everything my mother tried to fake—and somehow never quite managed. Weathered wooden floors that have been polished by decades of footsteps. Mismatched furniture that somehow coordinates perfectly. Mason jars filled with wildflowers on every surface. Hand-sewn pillows with embroidered sayings about family.

It's not just a house. It's a fucking *feeling*.

The kitchen is straight out of some cottage-core Instagram feed, except nothing about it feels staged. A cast iron skillet hangs on the wall next to an arrangement of wooden spoons worn smooth with use. Copper pots dangle from a rack over a center island where a bowl of actual fresh-picked apples sits. Not the waxed, perfectly identical ones from high-end grocers—real apples with imperfections and character, with stems still attached and occasional leaf clinging to the skin. The whole room smells of cinnamon and yeast and something deeper—the scent of meals cooked with intention rather than obligation.

"This is..." I start, but I can't find the right words. My vocabulary fails me completely.

"A mess?" June laughs, putting on her apron—not a

decorative one, but a well-worn canvas thing with pockets and stains that tell stories. "I know it's not what you're used to. Nothing like those marble countertops I've seen in your mother's kitchen posts."

She suddenly looks self-conscious, glancing around her own kitchen like she's seeing it through my eyes—through the lens of someone whose breakfast nooks have been featured in Architectural Digest. I realize with a start that she's nervous—about what I think. About me. Savannah Ashby. The Instagram princess standing in her flour-dusted domain.

"No, it's beautiful," I say, meaning it more than I've meant almost anything in years. "It feels real." The word catches in my throat because that's exactly what it is—real in a way my entire childhood never was.

June's face softens, crow's feet crinkling at the corners of her eyes. "You know, I've looked at your pictures on Instagram for... well, since you were very small."

She busies herself pulling ingredients from the refrigerator—eggs that still have bits of straw clinging to the shells, butter in a ceramic dish rather than wrapped in foil.

"I'm twelve years older than you, so I even remember the day your mother started the account. She was posting dozens of pictures a day—that was back before reels and stories, when filters were new and exciting, when a single Valencia-tinted snapshot could transport someone from their cramped apartment into a world of prairie sunsets and designer children's clothes. I was completely addicted to your life, checking for updates between feeding my babies and hanging laundry, wondering what magical childhood moment Eleanor had staged for you that day."

I don't know what to say. Of course, I've met many people over the years who say similar things. But they were strangers in meet-and-greet lines or PR events, not a biker's wife with flour on her cheek and a family farm so authentic and desirable, it makes my chest hurt with wanting.

Not someone who could probably recreate my childhood better than I lived it.

"Your playhouse was custom-built, wasn't it? All wood, one-of-a-kind," June continues while chopping vegetables with practiced efficiency, her knife moving in a blur that speaks of years of feeding hungry mouths. "It was filled with these exquisite sets of real china, delicate teapots with hand-painted flowers, and that miniature oak table where all your dolls would gather for their daily tea parties. I remember studying those photos for hours, marveling at how meticulously arranged everything was—the tiny napkins folded just so, the microscopic sugar cubes in their porcelain bowl. I used to wonder how a little girl could be trusted around such fragile treasures without shattering them to pieces. Most children I know would have reduced that china to dust within minutes."

I nod, watching her hands work, remembering how many times I did break those tiny teacups and how quickly they were replaced before the next photo shoot.

"You had that miniature chicken coop too—the one with the painted shutters and that adorable little ramp where those three speckled hens would strut down for the camera. And there was always some perfect, impossibly cute baby animal in your arms—kittens with ribbon collars, fluffy ducklings waddling after you, or those downy chicks nestled in your cupped hands."

Yup. This was my life. And every single one of those pets were carefully selected to be photogenic, to complete the picture-perfect rural childhood fantasy everyone was buying into.

"They were rotated out," I say. Just because I need her to know. "When they grew too big or stopped being cute enough. Nothing stayed, June. Nothing was permanent. I'm not even sure any of it was real. I mean, it wasn't real. It was a stage, I know that. But there's a little part of my brain that wonders... maybe it was all made up. Just some Little-House fever-dream that only existed in Eleanor Ashby's living diorama.

"Yeah," June says. "I get it. Your life was something out of a storybook," She scrapes diced carrots into a bowl with the edge of her knife. Then she looks at me. "But that's all life is, Savannah. A story. It's nothing but a story. And I think your mother was brave."

"*Brave?*" I nearly snort.

"Yes. Brave. Because she had the guts to shape it into whatever she wanted. Now..." June pauses her chopping and looks at me, really looks at me, and I have the uncomfortable feeling that she sees more than I want her to. That this woman in her vintage house dress can see right through the carefully constructed facade to the hollow space behind it. "I get it. She stole your story to write hers. She plagiarized you, Savannah. You have every right to resent that. To pledge that you'll never do the same to your daughter.

But don't be one of those people who rebel for rebellion's sake. It's a waste."

We just stare at each other until it gets uncomfortable. She says, "Here," and hands me a knife. Then she pushes a cutting board toward me. "Make yourself useful. Those potatoes won't dice themselves."

I take the knife, grateful for something to do with my hands. I haven't actually prepared food in... I can't remember how long. There were always staff for that. Chefs who appeared and disappeared without names, leaving perfect meals that photographed well but tasted like nothing.

"I'll give you the tour after we get the food ready," June says, moving to check something in the oven. The smell of vanilla and cinnamon intensifies as she opens the door, revealing what looks like a cobbler bubbling with dark berries. "I've made sides and dessert to go with Havoc's ribs. The man thinks meat is the only food group, but the kids need vegetables. And us girls need dessert."

She winks at me. And I smile. And then we work in companionable silence for a few minutes. I'm sure my potato dicing is amateur at best—uneven chunks that would make any chef cringe—but June doesn't comment. She just sweeps them into a pot with a practiced motion.

"Your life is very photogenic as well," I finally break the silence, because it feels like I should say something. Because her kitchen makes me ache with a longing I didn't know I had.

June's smile is genuine, crinkling the corners of her eyes. "I'll take that compliment. Especially coming from

Savannah Ashby, queen of the perfect golden-hour shot."

The way she says my name—like it means something beyond me—makes me wonder who she thinks I am. Who everyone thinks I am. This woman who's watched me grow up through a carefully curated lens, who probably knows more about the fiction of my life than I know of the reality.

After we finish preparing the food, June leads me through the rest of the house, givin' me the tour. Each room feels lived-in and loved. Children's artwork hangs in frames next to family photos—not professional portraits, but candid snapshots of real moments. Books are stacked on bedside tables—actual books with dog-eared pages and cracked spines, not decorative hardcovers arranged by color for aesthetic appeal.

I comment on things. Genuine comments, only. June and her farmhouse are probably the most authentic things I've seen in years. So tell I her I like the mix-matched patterns of her linen sheets. I like the antique furniture and cotton rugs. I like the texture of her floors and the panes in her windows.

Little details that almost no one mentions. Most people, when they see a house they like immediately identify why they like it.

I am not most people when it comes to details like that.

I see everything.

And June seems to enjoy my compliments. Telling me little stories as we walk, about how this house matured its way into a home.

After the tour, we carry the food outside to picnic

tables set up under a wooden pavilion strung with simple white lights. Havoc is still at the grill, Legion beside him, both men talking in low voices that stop when we approach. Legion's eyes find mine immediately, checking in without words, his gaze searching for any sign of discomfort.

I'm fine, I try to telegraph back. More than fine. Something in me has settled here, in this place that feels more like home than the mansion I grew up in.

After we set down the dishes, June touches my elbow. "Let me show you the garden before we eat."

She leads me past the pavilion to a fenced area where vegetables grow in neat rows, some still flowering, others heavy with produce. Beyond that is a chicken coop—not the decorative, useless kind my mother set up for photos, but a real working one with chickens that scratch and peck and actually produce eggs that people eat.

"The kids take turns collecting eggs in the morning," June explains, opening the gate so I can peek inside at the roost boxes. "It teaches responsibility. And they learn where food comes from, not just that it appears in refrigerators by magic. That's what I tell Havoc, anyway." She laughs. "But the honest truth is... I wanted your life, Savannah. It was never gonna happen for me as a child—I came from a broken home. We were very poor. So it became my dream to make it happen for my kids." She throws up her arms. "That's what we did here. We created the dream."

I wonder how many people have little farms like this because of my fake life on social media. How many women saw my mother's carefully constructed fiction and tried to build it for real, not knowing it was all smoke and mirrors.

The thought is both flattering and horrifying.

June closes the gate and turns to face me directly. Her expression has shifted to something more serious, the farm wife veneer slipping to reveal steel underneath.

"Can I give you some advice? Biker woman to biker woman."

I'm not sure I qualify as a "biker woman," but I nod anyway, suddenly aware that June Dun is more than her apron and homemade pies.

"It's a commitment," she says, her voice dropping to ensure we're not overheard. "And once you make it, it's your life." She reaches for my wrist, turning it so the fresh tattoo is visible in the evening light. "This is nothing. It means nothing if you're not willing to have his back when the world comes for him. That's how Havoc and I make it work, twenty-three years and counting."

She holds my gaze steadily, her fingers still gentle but firm on my wrist. "I'm telling you this because I know that's what you're asking. How do we make this work? How does a woman like me end up with a man like him, and not just survive, but thrive?"

It *is* what I'm asking, though I hadn't put it into words even for myself. The question that's been burning in me since he saved me from Marcus.

June leans in closer, and whispers, "I will kill for him. He will kill for me. And both of us will kill for those kids. That's the level of loyalty it takes to make it work."

Her eyes never leave mine, and there's something in them that makes me believe every word. This woman, with her homemade pies and hand-sewn curtains, would end someone without hesitation if they threatened what's hers. Would bury a body under those perfect vegetable rows and serve dinner with the same hands.

And suddenly I understand something about this world I've stepped into.

It's not just about leather, and motorcycles, and danger.

It's about a kind of loyalty I've never experienced—not from my family, not from Marcus, not from anyone except maybe Legion.

It's about building something real in a world of lies, and protecting it at all costs.

CHAPTER 9
LEGION

Havoc watches June and Savannah as they make their way into the house. Then, once they're inside, he turns to me, meat tongs in hand. "I hope you know what you're gettin' in to, Legion. That woman you've got, she's not like the rest. And by 'the rest' I do mean any other fuckin' woman you've ever met."

"Tell me about it," I say, taking a pull of my beer. "You think I don't know that, Havoc? I've been in love with that woman since she was a twelve-year-old girl. I was fourteen when we started this… affair, I guess it is. She was my first. I was hers too. What we have isn't new. It's older than Hell itself and I know who Savannah Ashby is better than anyone else in this world."

"That's why I'm telling you this."

"Telling me what?"

"That if you want her, you had better be ready to fight for her. Because there ain't no Ashby in the world—and by Ashby, I mean rich-mother fucker, regardless of the last name—who will let their carefully cultivated family matriarch be swept off her feet by a man like you."

Before I can take offense, he puts up a hand.

"Or man like me. Men like us, Legion? We don't marry the fuckin' princess. We can fuck them, feed them, eat them out on the porch. But we don't *marry* them."

I look out at the setting sun—it's really low now. Maybe half an hour, it'll be gone and then there will be nothing but these fairy lights above our heads. A fantasy.

I look back at Havoc. "So? I mean, what am I supposed to do with that information?"

"I dunno," he admits, flipping a rack of ribs with practiced precision. "I'm just reminding you, it don't happen this way. There's gonna be a fight, Legion. And it's gonna be ugly. If you love this woman, you better be prepared to fight for her like your life depends on it. And if you're not willing to blow up every fuckin' bridge you ever crossed to keep her, well..." He gives me a sad look now. "Maybe you should cut your losses."

The scoff comes out automatically. But before I can launch into a rebuttal, the screen door creaks open. June and Savannah emerge carrying steaming dishes, both smiling about somethin' I missed.

The sight of Savannah in that dress, her hair catching gold in the setting sun, makes my chest ache where the brand sits raw against my skin.

"Hope you boys are hungry," June calls out. "Savannah's quite the cook."

Savannah catches my eye, a silent laugh passing between us. She can barely boil water. We both know it.

The women set down their offerings—corn bread, beans, some kind of potato salad—then disappear back toward the garden, voices trailing behind them like ribbons. Something about tomatoes.

I watch Savannah's hips sway as she walks away, the dress moving against her like a second skin. When I turn back, Havoc's watching me with the patient stare of a man who's seen this story before.

"That woman's got you wrapped around her finger so tight you're turnin' blue, brother." He takes a long pull from his beer. "And that's your business. But when it bleeds into club business? It becomes my business."

"I've never given the club a reason to doubt me." The words come out sharp, defensive. "Three years, Havoc. Three years in Whitefall and I never said a word. Not one fucking word."

"I know." He nods, respecting the sacrifice. "That's why you got your patch. That's why you got your brand. But loyalty ain't a one-time payment, Legion. It's a subscription service."

I laugh, but there's no humor in it. "So what? I'm supposed to pick? The club or her?"

"I'm not saying that." Havoc turns the ribs again, his movements controlled. Nothing wasted. "I'm saying you need to figure out how to balance them both. Because right now? You're failing."

"Fuck you."

"That vote was the first split we've had in years." Havoc doesn't even flinch at my anger. "Eight men voted against you. Eight brothers who bled with you, who would have died for you yesterday, decided your judgment was compromised. You know how rare that is?"

I do. And it burns worse than the brand on my chest.

"Votes are never unanimous," I counter, but my voice lacks conviction.

"Not on business decisions, no. But on family matters? They usually are." Havoc points the tongs at me. "And this was about a woman. An Ashby woman. With connections to every powerful family in three counties. With a fiancé who's the son of a goddamn state senator."

I look away, across the yard where Havoc's kids are playing some complicated game involving sticks and shouting. Normal life. Somethin' I've never had.

"And then," Havoc continues, lowering his voice, "your sister shows up with Colt fucking Ashby and a baby. At our gates. After we voted to protect Savannah. What the fuck was that?"

The question hangs between us like smoke. I wish I had an answer that made sense.

"I dunno," I finally admit. "I don't know what that was."

"Well, you better figure it out. Fast." Havoc's voice drops even lower, almost a growl. "Because this is *drama*, Legion. And the more it follows you across the Badlands gate, the more men will vote against you next time."

"Next time?"

"There's always a next time." Havoc looks at me

with something like pity. "And next time will be the time it counts."

The words land like body blows. I know he's right. The club operates on a balance—loyalty to the patch versus loyalty to the man. Right now, I'm tipping the scales in a dangerous direction.

"So what would you do?" I ask, hating how the question tastes.

Havoc sighs, looking suddenly older than his years. "I'd remember that the club was there before her, and it'll be there after. I'd remember that forty-seven men are watching how you handle this. And I'd find a way to make peace with the Ashbys before they bring the kind of heat that burns us all."

"Make *peace*?" I laugh bitterly. "After what they did to her?"

"Not saying *forgive*. I'm saying neutralize." Havoc glances toward the garden where the women's voices float back to us. "Find leverage. Find dirt. Find something that makes them back the fuck off for good. Because right now, all you've done is piss them off."

I take a long drink, letting the beer wash down the anger rising in my throat. The sun touches the horizon now, bleeding red across the sky. In the distance, I can see Savannah and June walking back, a basket of something between them.

"She's worth it," I say quietly. "Whatever comes."

"Maybe so." Havoc nods. "But is she worth Mercy losing her brother again? Is she worth forty-seven men losing their livelihood if the law comes down? Is she worth burning everything you built while you were inside?"

I don't answer because I don't trust what might come out of my mouth. The brand on my chest throbs with each heartbeat, a reminder of promises made and kept. Savannah's getting closer now, laughing at something June said, looking like she belongs here in this yard, in this life. With me.

"You're a good man, Legion," Havoc says, surprisin' me. "Better than most who wear the patch. But good men make bad decisions when their hearts get involved. And bad decisions in our world—they don't just hurt you. They hurt everyone standing behind you."

As I watch Savannah approach, I feel something between love and terror creep up my spine. I've spent my whole life fighting—for respect, for survival, for her. But this might be the first time I've understood what I stand to lose.

"Just think about it," Havoc says, lifting the ribs from the grill. "That's all I'm asking."

Savannah reaches us, her smile bright but her eyes questioning as they move between Havoc and me. She can sense the tension, read it in the set of my shoulders.

"Everything okay?" she asks, her fingers finding mine, squeezing gently.

"Just man talk," Havoc answers before I can, his voice suddenly light. "Boring stuff about motorcycle parts."

I force a smile, but my mind is racing through every possibility, every threat, every choice that led us here. Eight votes against. A sister with an Ashby baby. A woman wearing my mark while her family plots revenge.

"Dinner's ready," June announces, clapping her hands to summon the children.

As everyone moves toward the table, Savannah holds me back, her eyes searchin' mine.

"What's wrong?" she whispers.

I brush my thumb across her cheek, memorizing the feel of her skin. "Nothing," I lie. "Everything's perfect."

But Havoc's words echo in my head like a warning bell.

Next time will be the time it counts.

We sit around the wooden tables under the pavilion that acts like an outdoor kitchen while the sky bleeds out, red-gold light washing across the yard.

Dinner's served family-style—platters of ribs, corn on the cob, biscuits, and coleslaw passed from hand to hand. The Dun kids' faces glow in the setting sun, all six of them jostling for position and talking over each other.

"Dad, I landed the double jump today," the oldest boy says, barbecue sauce smeared across his chin.

"Did you check your suspension after?" Havoc asks, not missing a beat.

"Yes, sir. Just like you showed me."

The second boy pipes up. "I'm gonna try it tomorrow."

"Not until I check your bike first," Havoc says, pointing a rib bone at him. "You bend that frame again, and you're walking till Christmas."

I watch them, these outlaw children with their normal lives. The contradiction doesn't escape me. They pass bowls and argue about whose turn it is to feed the dog.

"Misty's gonna foal any day now," the oldest girl tells Savannah, eyes bright with excitement. "Dad says I can help this time."

"That's amazing," Savannah says, and I can hear the genuine interest in her voice. "What breed?"

"Quarter horse. We're breeding for barrels." The girl beams with pride. "I'm taking Starlight to the fair next weekend for the 4-H competition."

"Your first show?" Savannah asks.

"Third," the girl corrects. "But first time in the advanced division."

June serves seconds before anyone asks, fillin' plates that never quite empty. She moves with the efficiency of someone who's fed an army, which I suppose she has.

"Speaking of the fair," June says, wiping her hands on a dish towel, "it's next weekend. All the kids have projects. Ethan's showing his woodwork, Leila's got her photography, and of course, the horses." She looks at Savannah, then me. "You two should come with us. Make a day of it."

Savannah turns to me, a question in her eyes. I shrug, knowin' damn well that Savannah Ashby, who's spent her life in curated Instagram moments, would probably love a real county fair with its dirt, and sugar, and chaos.

"Sure," I say. "Sounds good."

Savannah's smile is worth whatever bullshit I'll have to endure. One of the Dun twins pipes up from the end of the table. "Do you really have demons inside you?"

he asks me, eyes wide. "Cuz Dusty at the gate says you do."

"Michael!" June scolds, but I wave it off.

"Just the one," I tell the kid, keeping my face serious. "Keeps me warm in the winter."

The boy considers this, nodding like it makes perfect sense, and goes back to his corn. Across the table, Havoc's eyes meet mine—a silent warning that this is exactly the kind of talk that spreads.

I don't give a fuck. Let them believe what they want.

Sometimes a reputation keeps you safer than a gun.

"Dad's building a Camaro," one of the boys tells Savannah. "'69. It's in the outbuilding by the stables."

"Restoration project," Havoc explains, almost looking embarrassed. "Something to keep my hands busy when I'm home."

"He won't let anyone touch it," June says with a smile. "Not even me."

"Some things a man needs to do himself," Havoc says, and I nod because I understand.

Some work is prayer.

Some work is penance.

Sometimes they're the same thing.

Dinner winds down as the light fades. We eat dessert bathed in the same comfortable conversation. And when that's over June stands. "Alright, time for bed," she announces. This is met with a chorus of groans. "No arguments."

"Can we show Savannah the horses first?" the oldest girl asks.

"Another time," June says firmly. "Now scoot."

I watch them file inside, these children with their outlaw father and their normal lives. They each stop to kiss Havoc goodnight, even the oldest boy who's trying so hard to be a man. June follows them in, promising to return once they're settled.

Havoc pulls out two beers and a bottle of whiskey, settin' them on the table between us. Savannah takes a beer. I shake my head at both, pulling out my cigarettes instead.

"Mind?" I ask, tapping the pack.

"Just stay downwind of the house," Havoc says. "June'll have my ass if the kids smell it."

I light up, taking that first deep drag that feels like salvation. The nicotine hits my bloodstream as I exhale toward the darkening sky. Stars are coming out now, one by one, pinpricks in the black canvas above us.

"How'd you and June meet?" Savannah asks, taking a sip of her beer.

Havoc leans back in his chair, a smile softening his usually hard face. "Army. We were both stationed in Germany. She outranked me."

"Still does," I mutter, and Havoc laughs.

"Damn straight." He pours himself a finger of whiskey. "Third date, she described this life to me. This exact one we're living. The land, the house, the kids, all of it. Asked if it was my idea of paradise."

"And you said yes," Savannah fills in.

Havoc nods. "I said it was. She said, 'Let's make it happen.'"

I take another drag, once again studyin' the stars. In my head, I'm wondering how this squares with the

Badlands patch on his cut, with the gun room, with the blood I know he's spilled.

This little slice of heaven doesn't come cheap, and it doesn't come clean.

June returns, sliding into the chair beside Havoc. She must read the question on my face because she answers before I can ask it.

"This world doesn't owe you shit," she says, her voice suddenly harder than it's been all night. "If you want something, you have to take it. If you have a dream, you have to make it."

"And in order to make it, you need family. That's what the club is," Havoc says, looking directly at Savannah now. "*Family*."

I grunt in agreement, liftin' my cigarette in a mock toast. "To fuckin' family."

Family is Mercy waiting for me at the clubhouse.

Family is Destiny driving away with an Ashby baby in her arms.

Family is the men who voted to keep Savannah safe, and the eight who didn't.

Family is the weight that keeps you breathin' when you want to stop.

It's not perfect.

It doesn't have to be perfect.

It just has to be enough.

CHAPTER 10
SAVANNAH

Saying goodbye to June and Havoc feels like more of a somber affair than it should when it comes time to leave. It was a nice night. Their farm is quaint and lovely. Their children full of life and spark.

I want those things.

I want the small, lived-in house filled with things that have been collected over the years and come with experiences. I want the kids too. Maybe not six, but I can definitely see myself with a pack of them.

But it's June and Havoc's relationship that I find the most desirable.

Also, the most out of reach.

Twenty-three years they've been together. Twenty-three years they've pledged allegiance to each other. Stuck it out through the births, and deaths, and all unseen things that come with life.

And that's not even counting all the things that come with outlaw biker life.

I will kill for him. He will kill for me. And both of us will kill for those kids.

The words echo in my head as Legion revs the bike and we pull away from the farmhouse. I watch June's silhouette in the doorway, her hand raised in a simple goodbye. She doesn't wave it back and forth like most people do. Just holds it up, steady, like a promise.

Could I do that? Kill for Legion?

I wrap my arms tighter around his waist as we hit the main road, the wind whipping around my helmet. His body is warm against mine, solid. Real.

Maybe, under the right circumstances, I would kill someone for Legion. If it was in the moment and it was Legion's life or someone else's... I think I could do it.

But I felt there was something more to what June was saying.

Or rather, not saying.

Kill for him. It could be literal. But it doesn't have to be. I think I heard those words between the lines. The sacrifice. The willingness to burn everything else down if that's what it takes.

To choose him, over and over, when the world gives you every reason not to.

PROPERTY OF DEMON. It's not just ink. It's a declaration. A promise.

But is it one I can keep?

The night air is cool, and Legion is warm, so I let go of all my thoughts and just enjoy the ride back to Badlands. The rumble of the engine vibrates through me, and I press my helmet against Legion's leather-clad back. For now, this is enough. This moment. This man. This choice.

We pull into the compound, the gates opening without Legion having to slow down. The prospects recognize his bike. They know who belongs.

The clubhouse is still alive when we arrive, music spilling out the open door, laughter punctuating the night air. Legion parks his bike in line with the others, and I notice how perfectly it fits—like a puzzle piece sliding into place.

I wonder if I'll ever fit that seamlessly.

We get off the bike, and I hand him my helmet. Our fingers brush, and it's like electricity. Even after everything—the public claiming, the tattoo, the drama—I still feel that spark.

I hope I always will.

Legion takes my hand as we walk inside. Heads turn our way. Not everyone, just a few. Watching. Always watching.

I recognize most of the faces now. Have a story to tell about them too.

Chains, who marked me with Sharpie before I got the real ink. Diesel, who fed me shots. Brick, who called the vote that let me stay. Mama Jo, who organized the gifting. Ratchet working on the bikes. Butch and his guns.

One day. That's how long I've been here.

What will the backside of twenty-three years look like if I stay?

Will I be like June? Strong and certain, with a home full of laughter and weapons hidden in every room? Will Legion and I have children with his wild hair and my blue eyes? Will I still feel this pull, this certainty that despite everything—my family, my inheritance, my carefully curated life—this is where I'm supposed to be?

Yes. I think it will look like that. Today feels like a preview.

A moment of clarity in a sea of chaos.

Legion nods at Diesel, who raises his beer in acknowledgment. No words needed. That's another thing I've noticed—these men communicate in silences, in the spaces between words. It's so different from the world I come from, where everything is performance, where words are weapons and shields all at once.

Legion tugs my hand, leading me toward the stairs. I follow without hesitation. This is new for me—this *willingness* to be led. I've spent my whole life being directed—posed for cameras, dressed for events, scripted for interviews—but never truly following someone by choice.

The bunkhouse hallway is quiet compared to the bar below. Our boots echo on the worn wooden floor.

Yesterday, Room 3 was Legion's room.

Today, it's ours.

The door creaks as he pushes it open.

It's still sparse. Still feels temporary. But now there's a piece of me here too. My hairbrush on the milk crate. My borrowed clothes folded neatly on the footlocker.

Legion closes the door behind us, and the music from downstairs becomes a distant thrum. He doesn't turn on the light. Doesn't need to. Moonlight spills through the small window, painting silver stripes across the bed.

"Shower?" he asks, his voice low.

I nod, suddenly unable to speak. There's something

different in his eyes tonight. Something that wasn't there before. I can't name it, but I feel it—a shift, a deepening.

The bathroom is tiny, but functional and connected to his room. We both take off our boots before entering. The tiles are cold beneath my feet as Legion turns on the water, steam quickly filling the small space.

We undress each other slowly. No rush now. No audience. No desperation.

Just us and eternity, all living together in the same space.

The water is hot against my skin, a welcome contrast to the cool night air. Legion steps in behind me, closing the flimsy curtain. His hands find my waist, steady and sure.

While the sex over the past twenty-four hours has mostly been desperate and rushed—like we were about to be ripped apart, every time the last time—this is different.

His lips find mine, and there are no words. No dirty talk, no declarations, no promises neither of us can keep. Just kisses, deep and consuming. His hands trace my body like he's memorizing it, like he's afraid I might disappear if he closes his eyes.

I feel everything. The water cascading down our bodies. The slight sting where my tattoo is still healing. The press of his chest against mine, his heartbeat strong and steady under his brand, still raw and red, but looking more and more like it belongs there as the days pass.

When he hoists me up, my spine meets the cool tile wall as I instinctively lock my legs around his waist, our bodies finding each other with practiced familiarity. When he puts his hard cock in me, the connection makes me gasp against his mouth.

And when he starts fucking me, it's in deliberate, unhurried movements.

His forehead pressed to mine as our breathing creates its own rhythm in the steamy air between us.

He cradles my breasts with a reverent hand, his thumb and forefinger twisting my nipple with a gentle pressure that sends electricity coursing through me, a delicious counterpoint to the steady rhythm of our bodies.

His cock inside me is hard and insistent, even though the fucking is not rushed.

"Fuck, Savannah," he breathes against my neck, his voice rough with restraint. "You feel so goddamn good."

I can't form words. Can only moan in response as he hits that perfect spot inside me. My head falls back against the tile, eyes closing as water streams down my face, my neck, between our bodies where we're joined.

He adjusts his grip, one hand sliding to cup my ass, the other braced against the wall. The new angle makes me gasp, a sharp intake of breath that echoes in the small space.

"Look at me," he commands, and my eyes fly open. His are dark, intense, focused entirely on me. "I want to see you."

It's almost too much—the eye contact, the fullness, the way he's taking his time when I know he could just take what he wants. But I don't look away. I hold his gaze as he rocks into me, each thrust deliberate, measured, devastating.

My orgasm builds slowly, a warmth spreading from where we're connected, radiating outward. I can feel it coming, like a wave gathering strength offshore.

"Legion," I whisper, my voice barely audible over the sound of the water. "I'm close."

His rhythm doesn't change, but something in his eyes does—a flash of satisfaction, of pride. "Not yet," he says, and suddenly he's pulling out, setting me down on shaky legs.

I make a sound of protest, but he silences it with a kiss, deep and consuming. When he pulls back, he's smiling—that rare, genuine smile that transforms his face.

"On your knees," he says, and it's not a request.

I sink down without hesitation, the tile hard beneath my knees. The water hits my back now, streaming over my shoulders. Legion looks down at me, his cock hard and glistening. He grips his shaft, brushing the tip against my lips.

This should feel demeaning. In another life—the one where I lived every day as the little Ashby princess, and with another man, one like Marcus who only wanted to take—it would be.

But here, now, on my knees for Legion Kane, it feels like power. Like a choice.

I open my mouth, flick my tongue over his tip—all the while looking him dead in the eyes. My lips pucker around the head of his cock and I take him in slowly. His hand comes to rest on the back of my head, not pushing, just present.

I love watching him like this—the way his stomach muscles tense, the way his jaw clenches, the flutter of his pulse visible in his throat. I love knowing I'm the one doing this to him, breaking down the walls he keeps so carefully constructed.

I work him with my mouth and hand in tandem, setting my own pace. He lets me, though I can feel the restraint in the trembling of his thighs, the way his fingers flex against my scalp.

"*Fuck*," he groans, his eyes barely open now.

This single word a rumble of desire that I feel all the way down to my pussy. I've reduced him to this—to broken words and gasping breath.

I suck him in, taking him deeper, and his hand tightens in my hair. Not painful, just urgent.

"That's it," he says, his voice strained as he rocks forward into my throat. "Just like that."

The praise is erotic. Addictive. I want more. I redouble my efforts, using everything I've learned about what he likes. The water continues to cascade over us both, steam filling the small bathroom, making everything feel dreamlike and unreal.

Except this *is* real. This man, this moment—this is my choice.

This is what I want the backside of twenty-three to look like.

I pull back slightly, looking up at him through my lashes. His eyes are hooded, pupils blown wide with desire. I hold his gaze as I run my tongue along the underside of his cock, slow and deliberate.

A muscle jumps in his jaw.

"You're going to kill me," he says, and there's something almost like wonder in his voice.

I smile around him, then take him deep again. His

breath hitches, and I feel a surge of power. This is what June was talking about, I think. This willingness to give everything. To take everything. To be exactly who we are with each other, no pretense, no performance.

His hand guides me now, setting a rhythm that's just on the edge of too much. I follow it willingly, eagerly. My jaw aches, my knees hurt against the hard tile, but none of that matters compared to the sounds he's making, the way his body responds to mine.

"Savannah," he warns, his voice tight. "I'm gonna blow down your throat if you don't—."

He doesn't finish because I don't stop. Don't want to. I want all of him, every part he's willing to give.

His hand tightens in my hair as he comes with a groan that echoes off the tile walls. I take everything, swallowing around him, my eyes never leaving his face.

When he's spent, he pulls me to my feet, kissing me deeply despite where my mouth has just been. It's filthy and intimate and perfect.

"Your turn," he murmurs against my lips, and before I can respond, he's lifting me again, pressing me against the wall.

His fingers find me immediately, and I'm still so close from before that it takes almost nothing—just a few expert strokes and I'm coming apart, my nails digging into his shoulders, his name a broken sound on my lips.

We stay like that for a long moment, foreheads pressed together, breathing each other's air as the water begins to run cold. Legion reaches behind me to turn off the shower, and the sudden silence is deafening.

"I could get used to this," I say, not entirely meaning to speak aloud.

His eyes meet mine, serious now. "To what?"

"This," I gesture vaguely between us. "You. Me. Us."

Something flickers across his face—too quick to name. "You say that now," he says, helping me out of the shower, wrapping a towel around my shoulders. "But you haven't seen what this life really is yet."

I want to argue, to tell him I've seen enough. The violence, the loyalty, the way they operate outside the law but still have their own code.

But I know he's right. One day at the compound doesn't make me an expert.

One night with his brothers doesn't make me family.

I wrap the towel around myself, watching him as he dries off. His movements are efficient, practiced. No wasted motion. Everything Legion does has purpose.

"What?" Legion asks, catching me staring.

"I love you. That's all."

He freezes, towel in hand, water droplets still clinging to his skin. He doesn't say it back. Doesn't need to. I can see it in the way his eyes change, the way his body stills completely.

"I know you think I don't understand what I'm getting into," I continue, words tumbling out now. "That I'm just playing dress-up in your world. The little Ashby princess trying on outlaw life like it's another Instagram filter."

I step closer to him, close enough to feel the heat radiating from his skin.

"But I'm not naive, Legion. I grew up in a war zone

too—just one with better furniture." I laugh, but there's no humor in it. "You think your demons are so special? So unique? At least yours are honest about what they are."

My hand finds his chest, palm flat against the brand that marks him as Badlands. As brotherhood. As belonging.

"I know I'll fail you," I whisper, and his eyes narrow slightly. "Not because I want to. Not because I'm looking for an exit strategy. But because I'm human, and damaged, and sometimes I'll make choices that hurt us both."

I take a deep breath, steadying myself.

"I might fail you once. I might fail you a dozen times. But when I do—when you're at that breaking point, when you're ready to give up on me—I need you to remember this moment."

My fingers trace the outline of his brand, careful not to press too hard on the healing skin.

"Remember me, standing here, telling you that I am yours. That this—" I lift my wrist, showing him my tattoo, "—isn't just ink. It's a promise."

Legion's hand covers mine, pressing it more firmly against his chest so I can feel his heartbeat, strong and steady.

"I will fight for us," I continue, my voice gaining strength. "I will fight my family, your club, the whole fucking world if I have to. Because I want to make it to the backside of twenty-three with you, Legion. I want to see what we look like when we're old and gray and still choosing each other every single day."

I rise up on my toes, bringing my face closer to his.

"And if that means burning down everything I was supposed to be, then hand me the matches. Because I've spent my whole life being what other people needed me to be. The perfect daughter. The social media darling. The political trophy."

My hands frame his face now, holding him like something precious.

"But with you, I'm just Savannah. And that's enough."

Legion's eyes are so intense they almost burn, searching my face like he's looking for the lie, the angle, the hidden agenda.

He won't find one.

"I know what power looks like, Legion. I was raised in it. Groomed for it. I know how to smile for cameras while plotting behind my eyes. I know how to say the right things to the right people to get exactly what I want."

My thumb traces his bottom lip, feeling the slight roughness there.

"But I've never wanted anything the way I want you. Never needed anything the way I need us."

I let my hands fall to my sides, suddenly vulnerable in a way that has nothing to do with my nakedness.

"So yes, I'm choosing this life. I'm choosing you. With my eyes wide open. Knowing it will be hard, and messy, and sometimes dangerous. This isn't a game to me. It's not a rebellion, or a phase, or something to post about. It's my life now. *Our life.*"

I take a deep breath, steadying myself for what I need to say next.

"And I need you to believe that. Not because I say it, but because you feel it. Here." I place my hand over his heart again. "Where it matters."

CHAPTER 11
LEGION

Twenty-four hours ago we were trying to escape kidnappers.

Now Savannah has my name tattooed on her wrist, my sister had a baby with Colt Ashby, Mercy has a job working in the laundry, and Savannah is standing in front of me naked, telling me she's gonna get it wrong, but I should not give up on her. Because in the end, she'll get it right.

The silence stretches between us, filled only with our breathing and the distant sound of music from downstairs. Savannah has laid herself bare in ways that have nothing to do with skin, and now she waits, exposed and vulnerable, for my response.

My hand covers hers where it rests on my chest. I curl my fingers around her wrist, thumb brushing over the fresh tattoo. My touch is gentle, almost reverent.

"You think I don't know who you are?" I say, my voice low and rough. "You think I don't see you, Savannah?"

I pull her closer, one arm wrapping around her waist.

"I've been watching you since we were kids. I know exactly who you are. The real you—not the one your mother created for her cameras. Not the one Cash tried to sell to the highest bidder. Not the one Marcus thought he could own."

My fingers thread through her damp hair, cradling the back of her head.

"You're the girl who sang 'Ave Maria' in an abandoned grain silo because she thought no one was listening. You're the woman who rode bareback across Ashby land to meet me even though it could cost her everything."

My forehead dips down to touch hers, our breath mingling.

"You're right—you will fail me. And I'll fail you too. That's what people do. They fuck up. They hurt each other. They make mistakes."

My thumb traces her bottom lip.

"But the backside of twenty-three?" I laugh, because even though this is the first time I've ever heard that phrase, I know exactly what she's talking about. June and Havoc. What they have is special, and good, and real. And they fought hard for it. For each other.

And when she uses those words to me, that's what's she saying.

"The backside of twenty-three isn't about never failing. It's about failing and getting back up. Together."

I kiss her. I kiss her soft, and sweet, and tender. And when I pull away, I feel something I've never felt so acutely before in my life.

I feel vulnerable.

Love does that to you.

It pulls out the rug, takes everything, and dares you to still want it.

"I don't need you to burn down the world for me, Savannah. I just need you to stay. Even when it gets ugly. Even when it gets hard."

I find her wrist again and rub my thumb across the letters. Feeling the little scabs as I take in the red rings leftover from being bound to a bed by a man who thought he could buy her. Own her. It's evidence, these marks. Both of them. The tattoo and the remnants of captivity.

"This doesn't make you mine," I say. Rubbing her wrist. "You do. *You* make you mine. Every day. Every choice. Every time you look at me like you're lookin' at me right now. That's why you belong to me, Savannah. Because you choose to."

"Good. Because that's not what this is about," Savannah says. "This isn't about the ink, or the jacket, or even the claiming. It's about the quiet moments. The choices no one sees. The silent agreements we make with each other. And I know—I feel it, Legion. I feel it in my soul that the tryin' times that are comin' will test me and I will fail. But if you…" She swallows, struggling for words. "If you just remember that I made this promise. If you let me try again, whatever that means. I will not let you down."

I lean in and kiss her again. "Darlin'," I whisper into her mouth. "I can live with that vow."

Then I lead her out of the bathroom, still wet, but not caring, and I get in bed, pulling her in next to me.

I turn on my side, wrapping my arms around her waist, her perfect round ass pressed up against my cock—which is hard again, but there's time for that tomorrow.

And when she lets out that breath—the final breath for day one on the near side of twenty-three, I match her.

The near side is where all the danger is.

That's where we exist right now.

But her promise is enough to still me, and moments later, we're asleep.

In the black space between time, I dream.

Not dreams of peace, but of war.

Always war.

The eternal battle carved into my flesh, now etched into my sleeping mind.

In the beginning was darkness upon the face of the deep. And then came light—terrible, judging light that showed all things as they truly were.

Not as comfort, but as sword.

Flames lick upward from the depths, consuming everything in their path.

Faces form in the smoke—familiar faces, forgotten faces.

Some I know.

Some I've lost.

Some I've killed.

The fire speaks with many tongues, telling stories of what was, and what will be.

It whispers the name I've tried to forget.

My name is Legion: for we are many.

The flames rise higher, consuming flesh, and bone, and memory.

Nothing escapes the fire.

Not innocence.

Not guilt.

Not love.

Especially not love.

I am the archangel with the sword.

I am the beast with the horns.

I am the watchers with sealed beaks.

I am the skulls in their bone court.

I am the hands reaching through flame.

I am all of them.

For we are many.

CHAPTER 12
SAVANNAH

Someone's shouting.

No—several someones.

The sound filters through the thin walls, bounces down the hallway, seeps under the door. Voices rising and falling like waves crashing against rocks.

Angry waves.

Urgent waves.

Down below, a bike is revving.

Then another.

Doors banging.

Voices.

With the pillow now over my head, I burrow deeper into the mattress, trying to escape the noise and the light filtering through the blinds.

My head is pounding. Last night wasn't exactly wild, and I didn't drink much, but my crazy life is catching up to me and I'm desperate to go back to sleep.

But it's so fuckin' hot in here. Did the AC give out?

Beside me, Legion moans.

"What time is it?" I mutter, voice raspy and unfamiliar.

He doesn't answer.

I roll over, reaching for him, my fingers searching for the familiar warmth of his skin, the raised edges of his tattoos. My hand meets heat—intense heat—and I pull back instinctively.

Suddenly, I'm wide awake. Sitting up, looking down at him.

"Legion?" I whisper.

He's burning up. That's why I'm so hot. His skin radiates fever like a furnace, the sheets beneath him damp with sweat. His chest rises and falls too quickly, breath shallow and uneven.

"Legion?" I touch his shoulder gently, trying to rouse him. "Hey. Wake up."

Nothing. Not even a flicker of his eyelids.

"Legion." I shake him, gentle at first, then with more force. "Legion, come on. Open your eyes."

His head lolls to the side, unresponsive. Panic starts to build in my chest, a tight, squeezing sensation that makes it hard to breathe.

Outside, the commotion grows louder.

Someone shouts an order.

Boots pound across gravel.

A door slams.

I tune it out, focusing only on Legion. I slide out of bed, grab the first things I find—a pair of shorts, one of Legion's t-shirts—and pull them on quickly. Back at his side, I press my palm to his forehead. He's so hot, his skin slick with sweat.

"Legion!" I'm shaking him harder now, desperation creeping into my voice. "Please wake up. *Please*."

That's when I see it—his brand. The Badlands "B" they burned into his chest the night of his patching ceremony. It's angry red, swollen, with yellow-green pus oozing from the center. The skin around it is hot to the touch, streaked with red lines that spread outward like poison.

"Oh, my god." My stomach lurches. "*Legion*. Legion, wake up." I'm saying his name over and over, like a prayer, like if I say it enough times he'll have to answer. "Legion, please. Please wake up."

He doesn't move. Doesn't respond. His breathing remains shallow, too fast.

A siren bleeps outside, cutting through the shouting. One short burst, then silence.

I rush to the window, pushing aside the blinds. Down in the compound, chaos unfolds. Men running in every direction, shouting to each other. And at the gate a sheriff's cruiser, lights flashing.

Two deputies standing beside it, hands on their holsters.

What the fuck is happening?

I turn back to Legion, who looks like death itself, then to the window again. I can't process both emergencies at once. Legion needs a doctor, but there are cops at the gate, and no one's coming to help us.

I need to find someone. Anyone.

I bolt from the room, bare feet slapping against the worn floorboards as I race down the hall, then take the stairs two at a time, nearly colliding with a young man at the bottom.

"Where's Diesel?" I demand. "Or Brick? Or—anyone? Legion's sick. Really sick."

The kid just shakes his head, pushing past me, running toward the front door.

The main room is a blur of leather cuts and weapons. Men move with purpose, faces grim, no one even glancing my way. I spot Mama Jo near the bar and rush toward her.

"Mama Jo! Please—it's Legion. He's burning up with fever. His brand is infected. I can't wake him up."

She barely looks at me, eyes fixed on something across the room. "Not now, girl. We've got bigger problems." She pushes me aside, moving away.

"Wait!" I grab her arm. "You don't understand. He needs a doctor. He's—"

"I said not now!" She yanks free, disappearing into the crowd.

Everyone is shouting. Orders, questions, curses. No one's listening. No one cares that Legion might be dying upstairs. I stand in the middle of it all, invisible, helpless.

The rage builds inside me—sudden, white-hot, overwhelming.

"STOP!" I scream, loud enough that my voice cracks. "LISTEN TO ME!"

The room doesn't go silent—this isn't a movie—but heads turn. Eyes find me. For a moment, I have their attention.

"Legion is sick," I say, forcing my voice to stay steady. "Really sick. He needs a doctor. *Now*."

A few men exchange glances. Someone mutters something I can't hear. But before anyone can respond,

Brick emerges from the open front door, face like thunder.

"Where the fuck is Legion?" he demands, eyes locking on me.

Finally. Someone who'll listen.

"He's upstairs," I say, relief flooding through me despite Brick's anger. "He's burning up with fever. The brand is infected. I can't wake him up. He needs—"

"We've got bigger problems," Brick cuts me off, echoing Mama Jo's dismissal. "Sheriff's here with a warrant. He needs to get his ass up and talk to them."

My relief evaporates. "You're not listening. He can't get up. He's unconscious. His brand is infected—it's oozing pus. He needs a hospital."

Brick's eyes narrow, assessing whether I'm telling the truth. Then he swears, a string of words that would make my mother's ghost faint.

He heads to the stairs, his long legs taking them four at a time. I follow him back to Room 3, a stream of men trailing behind us. When Brick sees Legion, even he looks worried. He tries shaking him, slapping his face lightly, calling his name. Nothing works.

"Fuck," he mutters. Then, to the room at large: "Sheriff's got a warrant to search the compound for Mercy Kane."

My heart drops. "What? Why?"

"Someone called social services. Reported that Mercy was staying here." Brick's eyes are cold. "If we don't turn her over, they'll search the place." He gives me a look that makes my skin crawl. "They are *not* coming in to search this compound."

Then he points to Roach, who's standing just outside the door. "Go get the girl."

The implication hits me like a slap. They're going to hand Mercy over to the authorities. While her brother lies here, possibly dying.

"Wait," I say, panic rising again. "Legion needs to go to the hospital. Now. Before—"

"I'll take him." One of the younger men steps forward. "I can drive them to the hospital in Terry. It's closest."

Brick nods. "Fine, you take care of them, Dusty. Call me when you get there and give me an update." Then Brick turns to Ledger. "Just in case they come in, go make sure everything is put away properly."

"On it, Boss," then Ledger rushes out, his boots thumping on the hallway and stairs.

From outside comes a high, panicked scream. "Legion! *LEGION!*"

A child's scream.

I rush to the window. Down in the yard, Roach and another club member are dragging Mercy toward the gate. She's fighting them, kicking and screaming her brother's name, small body twisting against their grip.

And beyond that, parked just outside the gate is a truck. A truck I know well because it's got the Ashby logo on the door.

Cash's truck.

Everything clicks into place with sickening clarity. And in that same moment, his eyes slide up to my window.

He smiles at me. Grins. Tips his stupid fucking Stetson.

He did this.

Cash did this.

Called social services about Mercy.

Created this mess to make us pay.

Brick appears beside me at the window. He sees the truck too. "You're one of us now," he says, voice low. "We voted and you got the ink to prove it. But that also means the club comes first from now on, Not Mine."

He gestures to Legion. "Get your shit. Take him to the hospital. And find somewhere else to stay." His mouth twists. "I hear there's a perfectly nice new trailer on twenty acres outside Drybone."

Then he's gone, leaving me alone in Room 3 with a possibly dying Legion and only some kid named Dusty to help me.

My world narrows to this moment.

Legion burning with fever.

Mercy screaming his name as she's dragged away.

Cash waiting outside, ready to take her God knows where.

And me.

The backside of twenty-three laughs in my face.

You think you know what trouble is, bitch, the near side asks.

You think you know what sacrifice is, the near side taunts.

You think you have what it takes to keep him alive, let alone still in love with you after two decades, the near side sneers.

Fool.

Fantasy.

But I flip the near side of twenty-three off and give Dusty a nod as I pick up Legions jeans and start pulling them up his legs.

"Let's fuckin' go."

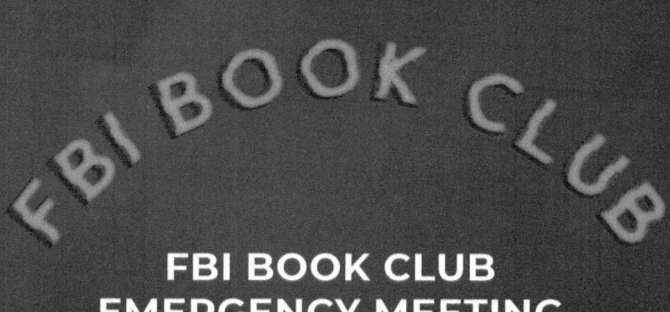

FBI BOOK CLUB
EMERGENCY MEETING

FBI BOOK CLUB
EMERGENCY SESSION TUESDAY
SCIF-CHAT (UNAUTHORIZED)
Assignment: Scars and Promises (Book of Legion #3) by
JA Huss
Transcript — CLASSIFIED (Castillo insists)

[9:00 AM — AGENT: KOWALSKI has started the meeting]
[9:00 AM — AGENT: KOWALSKI has flagged meeting as: EMERGENCY]
[KOWALSKI VISUAL — parked car, overhead light on, box of Honey Nut Cheerios in lap]

Kowalski: I am calling this meeting to order. I don't care that it's Tuesday.

[9:01 AM — AGENT: MARSH has entered the meeting]

[MARSH VISUAL — outdoor shooting range, ear protection around neck, Glock on counter]

Marsh: *Unmute.* Who's dead? *Mute.*

Kowalski: LEGION MIGHT BE! 💀 🩸 🗡

[9:01 AM — **AGENT: CASTILLO** has entered the meeting]

[CASTILLO VISUAL — interrogation room, suspect visible in background, hands cuffed to table]

Castillo: Three minutes. Go.

Kowalski: CASH CALLED CPS WHILE LEGION WAS CONVULSING. THE BRAND WENT SEPTIC. THEY DRAGGED MERCY OUT SCREAMING. HE TIPPED HIS FUCKING HAT CASTILLO HE TIPPED HIS FUCKING STETSON 💀💀💀 🩸🩸🩸 🗡🗡🗡

[9:02 AM — **AGENT: KAI** has entered the meeting]

[KAI VISUAL — outdoors, wind in hair, vast eroded badlands formations filling the entire background]

Kai: Hey. Got the ping. What's the emergency?

Kowalski: KAI WHAT THE FUCK

Castillo: …

Marsh: *Unmute.* Are those the Terry Badlands? *Mute.*

Kowalski: WHAT'S THE — KAI YOU ARE STANDING IN MONTANA 😭🗡️🖤💀 💧🔪😰🥺

Kai: I had PTO.

Castillo: Those are my coordinates.

Kai: Your geographic profile was very thorough.

Castillo: [*to suspect, off camera*] Stop crying. This doesn't concern you.

Kowalski: I can't — the BRAND is ROTTING and Mercy is GONE and Kai is in MONTANA and Castillo has a MAN CRYING — is anyone going to talk about the BOOK or am I just GOING TO DIE HERE by MYSELF

Kai: So the grain elevator is real. I'm about a hundred yards from it right now. Corrugated metal, decommissioned, cottonwood line runs right along the creek bed exactly like she described—

Marsh: *Unmute.* The attachment rupture with Mercy replicates the original abandonment schema. Cash detonated years of therapeutic progress in one tactical— **[GUNFIRE — 3 rounds]** *Mute*

Kowalski: —and the scar tissue, they cut away so much the B isn't even READABLE anymore and he says it feels like something growing under his skin like he's being UNMADE 💀 💧 🖤 😩 which is a METAPHOR for—

Kai: —there's a trailer on the east side of the creek. Double-wide. Metal siding, timber accents. Looks newer than the surrounding structures. Someone lived here and left. Fridge is hanging open through the window—

Castillo: Condition of the trailer?

Kai: Solid. Weeds at the foundation. Maybe empty a year, two max. There's a porch—

Kowalski: —HE TIPPED HIS HAT. HE TIPPED HIS HAT LIKE HE WON. LIKE MERCY WAS JUST A CHESS PIECE. A NINE-YEAR-OLD WITH A BB GUN AND SAGE WALLS AND A HORSE LUNCH BOX AND HE USED HER LIKE A FUCKING PAWN 💀 🗡 💧 🔪🔪🔪🔪🔪

[9:06 AM — AGENT: DAVID has entered the meeting]
[DAVID VISUAL— office, tie loosened, slightly out of breath]
[9:06 AM — AGENT: DAVID has assumed MODERATOR role]
[9:06 AM — AGENT: DAVID has enabled Profanity Filter: Auto-Emoji Mode]

David: I ran three flights of stairs. Why is Kai in the

badlands? Why is there a suspect on Castillo's camera? Why is Kowalski eating cereal?

Kowalski: 💀 🗡️ 🖤 💧 🔪 😩 😭 🫥

David: That's not a sentence. Also — IA has deployed a new AI transcript scanner. Every meeting on this platform is being flagged and parsed for content violations starting THIS WEEK, which means everything we say—

Kai: —and about forty yards from the trailer there's an old cottonwood. Massive. And there are carvings on it.

David: —is being run through a sentiment analysis model that flags for, quote, "non-operational emotional engagement with fictional media on government time"—

Kowalski: CARVINGS??? 😩😩😩 🗡️🗡️🗡️ 🖤🖤🖤 💀 💀 💀

David: —which means LAST WEEK'S transcript where Kowalski said she wanted to—

Marsh: *Unmute*. Kai. Describe the carvings. **[GUNFIRE — 2 rounds]** *Mute*.

David: —"climb Legion like the grain silo he decorated" is NOW in an AI-generated behavioral report on my DESK—

Kai: Two letters. Maybe four. Deeply cut. Old. And

there's something crossed over them. Knife marks. Different depth than the original. Different weathering. Like someone came back angry.

David: —and I have to certify that this book club is "operationally adjacent" to maintain the meeting authorization, so if ANYONE could explain to me how tree carvings in Montana are—

Kowalski: 😫🗡🖤💀💧🔪💀😵⬜🖤🖤🖤💧💧💧💀💀💀💀💀💀💀 IF THOSE LETTERS ARE S AND L I AM FILING EMOTIONAL DISABILITY AND LISTING JA HUSS AS THE CAUSE OF INJURY

Castillo: [to suspect] I SAID stop crying. [to camera] Kai. Photograph macro. Wide shot relative to trailer. Include cottonwood line to creek.

David: IS ANYONE LISTENING TO ME ABOUT THE AI SCANNER?

Kowalski: NO 🔪

Marsh: *Unmute.* No. [GUNFIRE — 4 rounds, rapid] *Mute.*

Marsh: *Unmute.* Those were for Cash. *Mute.*

Castillo: No. I need to go. He's getting loud.

[CASTILLO AUDIO: Banging on interrogation room door]

Kai: No. But the light's shifting. I can almost read the cuts now.

David: I am filing a preemptive IA exemption for this entire group.

[9:09 AM — AGENT: DAVID has left the meeting]

Kowalski: HE SAID PREEMPTIVE. HE'S PROTECTING US. HE ✽✽✽ING LOVES US. 💀🖤💀🖤💀

[CASTILLO AUDIO: "No, STOP! I said I'd tell you EVERYTHING—"]

[9:09 AM — AGENT: CASTILLO has left the meeting]

Kai: Kowalski.

Kowalski: WHAT 🔪⚔️💀💧

Kai: Light just shifted. I can read the tree.

[silence]

Kowalski: …

Kai: There's an S. And there's something else. Could be an L. Could be a J. The cross marks are deep. Someone was angry when they did this.

Kowalski: 😩😩😩😩😩🔪🔪🔪🖤🖤🖤💀💀💀💧💧💧🔪🔪🔪🤢🤢🤢

Marsh: *Unmute.* She's been there. This isn't fiction. This is memory. **[GUNFIRE — 1 round]** *Mute.*

Kowalski: I am reading Book 4 in this parking garage RIGHT NOW. I have thirty-eight minutes before my shift and I do not CARE. 📖🔪🖤💀💧

Kai: I'm going to walk the creek bed. The last two miles. Where Earl drops him at the crossroads.

Kowalski: Walk it for him 🖤

Kai: …Yeah.

[9:11 AM — AGENT: KOWALSKI has ended the meeting]

[9:12 AM — AGENT: DAVID (text to group chat):] I am not part of this. But Kai — check the east bank for vehicle access.

[9:12 AM — AGENT: KOWALSKI (text to group chat):] 💀💀💀💀💀💀💀💀💀💀💀💀💀💀

[9:12 AM — SCIF-CHAT AUTO-SUMMARY: MEETING TRANSCRIPT COMPILED]

SMOKE & honey

Book of Legion ~ Badlands MC #4

New York Times Bestselling Author

JA HUSS

GET THE NEXT BOOK

Ponies and presents.
Princess in training.
Dynasty wealth.
Always on the outside lookin' in.
Some men weren't built to stay.

SMOKE AND HONEY

Where the right side of the tracks meets the wrong side of everything.

Inside the pages you can expect:

Outlaw Biker Romance
Rich Girl / Poor Boy
Property Of
Morally Gray / Anti-Hero MMC
Obsessed / Possessive MMC
Forbidden Love
Only Her
Only Him
Childhood Sweethearts
Touch Her and Die
Primal Spice
Secret Relationship

ABOUT THE AUTHOR

JA Huss is a scientist, New York Times and USA Today bestselling author. Her self-published romantasy Sparktopia was named an Audible Editors' Best of the Year selection in 2024, and several of her audiobooks have been nominated for the Audie and SOVA Awards. A 2019 RITA finalist, Huss has also had five books optioned for film and television.

www.ingramcontent.com/pod-product-compliance
Lightning Source LLC
LaVergne TN
LVHW090041080526
838202LV00046B/3913